I0572405

REAPER
WAR BROTHERS MC

BIANCA LEE WARD

ALSO BY BIANCA LEE WARD

BOMBER

War Brothers MC

I won't lose her again.

But our family secrets could tear us apart…

It's been ten years since I was forced to let Zara go. I joined the military and fought hard to forget her, but since I returned home to become our club's Sergeant at Arms, I've always watched from afar to make sure she's safe.

Now Zara is back in Crown Village on the anniversary of a traumatic event that changed her family forever. And I can't stay away.

I can see the longing for me in her eyes, yet she hesitates to get too close. She's scared to trust me again, and I don't blame her.

When new information linked to her family tragedy comes to light, I'm determined to help solve the mystery and find the answers she needs because the War Brothers MC protects our own.

But digging up the past means revealing secrets that someone wants to remain dead and buried. And when they're uncovered, they have the power to destroy our bond forever…

Grab a copy of Bomber now!

VIPER

War Brothers MC

I've got one month to convince her to be my wife…

Until I laid eyes on Sophie, I never planned on marriage. All that changed after our hot night together in Vegas.

Now she regrets our impulsive Vegas wedding and is demanding a divorce. But I'm not signing the papers. Hell no! I'll give up every single one of my womanizing ways for a woman like her.

Sophie thinks I'm only infatuated by her looks, except I see how everyone underestimates her. I'm not intimidated by her wealth, her modeling career, and the trail of broken hearts. What we have is different.

I've lived my whole life unable to feel anything thanks to my rough childhood, but for Sophie, I'll risk everything. Her rich father or the jealous women in my club aren't going to stand in my way.

If she wants a divorce, she'll have to spend one month with me at the War Brothers clubhouse. Sleeping in my bed.

Then we'll see if she still refuses to say I do...

Grab your copy of Viper now.

PLAYLIST

Nobody's Home — Avril Lavigne
Hurt The Same — Nowhere Left
Debonaire — Dope
Warrior — Demi Lovato
Scars — I Prevail
Face Down — The Red Jumpsuit Apparatus
Control — Zoe Wees
Glad You Came — The Wanted
Make Them Mine — Meyo
Dangerous Woman — Ariana Grande
Dark Horse — Our Last Night
Middle Of The Night — Loveless
Wonderwall — Oasis
Silence — Marshmellow, Khalid
I Want You To Know — Zedd, Selena Gomez
Look What You Made Me Do — Our Last Night
Here With Me — Dido
I Wanna Die — Nessa Barrett
Jump Around — House Of Pain
You Should See Me In A Crown — Billie Eilish
Bury Me With My Guns — Bobaflex
#1 Crush — Garbage
Finally — Amba Shepherd & Mikkas
Don't Stay — Linkin Park
Zombie — The Cranberries
Triggered — SkyDxddy
You Should Be Sad — Halsey
Final Warning — Skylar Grey
Your Guardian Angel — The Red Jumpsuit Apparatus

DEDICATION

Dear Dad,
I had to include rottweilers in at least one of my books
because I know how much you loved them. Give Conan, Jady,
Titan, Dara, Facey, and Ike a pat for me.
I love you always and forever.
Until we meet again x

PROLOGUE – SHE'S NOT MINE

Reaper

I want her.

Those curves. That smile. I've never been so attracted to a woman. I take a swig of my beer and watch as she talks to her sister, Elena. We are at Elena and Axle's wedding. The men mentioned Elena had a sister, but I have never seen her before today, and I know I won't be forgetting her anytime soon. She leans in, picks up her champagne, and takes a few sips. When she places it on the table, the strap of her dress falls from her shoulder, and all I want to do is taste her.

I readjust myself in my seat.

Viper elbows me. "You like her?" He gives Elena's sister a pointed look.

Bomber leans in from the other side of me, listening to our conversation.

"I do." I want her badly.

"Her name's Ava," says Viper.

I raise a brow, and he grins smugly.

"What?" he says with his hands up. "She's fucking hot, so of course I asked Axle about her."

My jaw clenches. The possessiveness shooting through me surprises me. I don't even know her. I glance at Bomber, and the side of his lip twitches like he's smothering a smirk. The observant bastard misses nothing.

"She's married," Viper chimes in. "Not that it means anything these days."

I lift my hand to my chin. "I wonder how committed."

"Axle didn't say, but he warned me to stay away. He said —and I quote—'I want to have sex with my wife tonight, and I don't want anyone fucking that up for me. So Ava's off limits.'" Viper's voice mocks Axle's.

Ava is still deep in conversation with Elena; then they laugh. The music is too loud, so I can't hear them, but it makes me curious as to what her laugh sounds like.

"Is her husband here?" I ask Viper.

He laughs. "It's the guy sitting next to Elena's mom at the table next to the bride and groom."

I peer at Elena's parents and see a man gulping half of his bottle of beer next to them. His eyes are on Ava.

"She's with the drunk?" I ask, shocked, remembering the man stumbling to the bar earlier.

"Yep. I couldn't believe it either. She's way too good for him."

I stare at the man who has what I want. He's average looking, nothing special.

"I saw him earlier, but I thought he was a family member."

I haven't seen him touch or kiss Ava or show any affection that would suggest they're married. If she was mine, I wouldn't be able to keep my hands off her. I'd want the world to know.

"Viper," Candy calls from the dance floor. "Come and dance with me."

His smile widens. "I'm coming." He stands. "Well, fellas, it's my time to shine."

Chuckling, I shake my head.

He fixes his hair like he's a peacock parading its feathers. "What? I've got moves."

"Yeah, okay, Justin Timberlake," I taunt.

He walks to Candy, puts his arm across her back, and dips her backward, lifting a brow and grinning at us. She lets out a squeal and laughs.

Demon's leaning back in his chair, looking at the dance floor. He doesn't look like he's watching people dancing; it's like he sees through them, as if his mind is elsewhere. He taps on the table, and even with his tattoos, bruises and scabs on his knuckles from the other night stand out.

I lean toward him and raise my voice. "You don't have to stay here."

He slowly turns his head with a wicked smile and then stands. He lifts his chin. "I'll see you back at the clubhouse later."

With a sharp nod, I watch as people step away from him, giving him room to move freely to the exit.

I make eye contact with Axle. He leaves a group and walks to us.

"Is Demon leaving already?" He looks at his watch. "It's still early."

"He looked bored, which is usually not good."

He sighs. "Good point."

"Is Ava really married?" I ask, hoping Viper got it wrong.

Axle's eyes widen. "You too?" His shoulders drop. "Just give me one night of wild sex with my wife. I don't want her in my ear saying that her sister had sex with a biker and got divorced over it." His voice is whiney.

Even though it's tempting, I respect Axle too much to do anything about it, but something claws inside of me. "You have my word."

He blows out a gush of air. Elena appears at his side. He looks at her, smiles, and puts his arm around her waist. "You owe me a dance."

She smiles back. "I thought you'd never ask."

He grabs her hand and leads her to the dance floor.

I search for Ava but can't find her. I sit upright in my chair, looking around. "She walked toward the restroom," says Bomber, like he read my mind. We've been friends for a long time. We know each other well.

"Thanks," I reply, my eyes turning to the hallway leading to the bathroom. I fidget in my chair, wanting to get up, but the discussion I had with Axle keeps me seated.

I may never see her again plays in my head. I've never felt a strong pull to a woman before, so I stop fighting myself and then stride toward the restrooms. I won't have sex with her anyway. I'm just curious.

As I get closer, she walks out. Her eyes are on her dress as she tries to pull up its cleavage. Her dress covers most of her boobs, but with big perfect tits like that, I don't know why she is bothering. She looks flawless the way it is.

She huffs when the dress won't cover her further. When she lifts her eyes, they widen when she sees me staring at her, and it's like someone has punched me in the gut.

"You're beautiful."

Freezing, Ava stares at me with wide eyes. She says nothing, but a blush creeps up her neck and to her face. She breaks eye contact as she picks at her dress. When she looks up at me, she smiles and her eyes glisten like she's holding back tears. "Thank you."

In my periphery, her husband approaches us with narrowed eyes, though swaying to the right. The warmth in my chest dissipates, and my body tenses and turns to stone. I glance at Ava, and when her eyes lock onto her husband, she gasps and steps away from me. Her breathing has picked up. Her shoulders have hunched over, and she looks scared.

I fucking hate it. Something isn't right.

When he reaches us, I can smell the alcohol on him. He looks me up and down with his glassy eyes, and I don't miss the tightness in his jaw.

His hand comes out to me. "Beau."

I shake his hand, noticing his firm grip. "Reaper."

He coughs. "Well, that's certainly a name you've got there."

I ignore him and look at Ava. She swallows thickly as her eyes keep darting between me and her husband.

"I'm ready to go, Ava. Your parents are leaving, too."

My eyes widen. No "are you ready to leave?" It seems like an order.

"You can stay with your sister. There are spare rooms available," I tell her.

He answers for her. "Ava's tired." Then he looks at her. "Aren't you?"

"Ah, yes," she replies and gives me a small smile. "But I appreciate the offer."

Beau grabs her arm. She flinches. My hands clench at my side.

"Have a good night," she says before they turn and leave.

It takes everything in me to stay still, to not rip her away from him. My gut churns.

Something isn't right; she fears him.

I close my eyes briefly. "She's not mine," I say to myself. "She's not mine."

ONE
CLIPPED WINGS

One Year Later

Ava

His loud snoring fills the room. I watch him closely as I sit up, then drag the duvet off me. When I turn to the edge of the bed, it causes pain to shoot up my side, making my eyes squeeze shut. When my feet hit the floor, I slowly stand, but the bed creaks. It makes my stomach drop. My eyes flick to him, but he's still asleep. I grab my phone from the night-stand. My feet pad on the floor as I tiptoe out of the room. My heartbeat is surging as I quietly pull the door shut.

Using my phone as a light, I move to the closet in the spare room, then reach up and grab the old beanie. I open it up to pick out the cash I've been saving. I take my jeans and a loose shirt off the hanger and get changed. I put on a black coat and leave the hood up to cover my head.

I grab the backpack with shaky hands and sling it over my shoulder. In the kitchen, I grab my purse and place the money inside.

I peek back once more before I open the front door and step outside.

Fresh air meets my face, making me shiver, but I know it's not just from the cold. I dart down the stairs, then run onto the road, even though every step brings me pain. I run as if someone is chasing me, and even though he's in bed, asleep, it still feels like he's here with me. I hope the fear leaves me, even if it means hiding away from him forever.

A few streets away, I reach an area surrounded by trees and bushes and pull my phone from my pocket and make a call, even though it fills me with shame.

When she answers, loud music and shuffling echoes in the background.

"Ava, is that you?"

My mouth goes dry. *I'm so weak.* I never used to be this person, and here I am, calling my younger sister for help.

"Ava?"

"Hey, Elena," I say through sniffling.

"Who's that calling?" a man asks.

"Shh . . . It's my sister," Elena says.

"What's wrong? Are you okay?" she asks, sounding worried.

For the first time, I say, "No. I'm not."

"What happened?"

My stomach plummets. A car rolls by, so I hide behind a tree, paranoid it could be him. "I need to get out of here," I whisper, my voice coarse.

There's a brief silence before she speaks. "What's he done?"

"Nothing, nothing. I just need somewhere to stay before I

get back on my feet, that's all." I'll quickly burn through that money I saved if I have to pay for accommodation.

"At one in the morning?"

I didn't think this through. She would have a lot of questions. I've had no contact with her since the wedding, and before that we had been distant for years.

She answers, "You can stay here, if you're okay with staying at a clubhouse because we haven't brought our own place yet."

My sister married a biker a year ago, and at any point, I would have said no way, but I will stay anywhere. "That's fine. I promise I won't stay long. It's just until I can get a job."

"Are you guys getting a divorce or something?"

Pausing, I close my eyes. "Something like that."

She sighs. "I'm glad you're getting out of that marriage. It felt like I lost you to him. You stopped calling."

She pays more attention than I thought.

"I'll catch a bus there. Can you tell me the address?"

"Don't be stupid. You have to tell me something."

I exhale through my mouth, knowing no makeup could hide the bruise on my face from yesterday afternoon.

"So am I meeting you at your house, or . . .?"

"No."

"I'm coming." I hear the male voice again.

I have met her husband only briefly, so I'm not sure how he will react.

"Where am I picking you up?"

I think he'll check public transportation for me if he wakes up. "Do you remember the park near my house?" I don't think he'll look for me at the park. I can get there from here without going on the road.

"At this time of night? Are you insane?"

"Please . . ." My voice is strained.

Again, she sighs. "Promise me you'll call if you see anything suspicious."

"I will."

"Okay, we will get there as soon as we can."

Relief floods me, and I make my way to the trail that leads to the park. Without the lights from the street, it's darker, so I turn on my phone's flashlight. Luckily for me, the dirt track has been cleared because the kids use it to ride their bikes through here.

It's eerily quiet as I walk through, and those intrusive thoughts flood my brain. I'm so pitiful that I've had to call my sister for help. I should have gotten out of the marriage sooner. I saw the red flags and talked to Mom about it, but she encouraged me to stay. I should have known better than to converse with her, but who else was I going to talk to? The only people Beau approved of were my parents.

My ankle rolls on unsteady ground, and I cry out in agony when I land hard. My hands burn from protecting my head and body from the fall. I sit up through a hissed breath and reach out for my phone, which slid under a small shrub. I wipe my hand on my coat to get rid of the dirt, and when I peer down, blood is trickling from the wound. I swap my phone to my bleeding hand to check the other, but it's fine.

When I pull my jeans up my calf, I see my ankle is swelling. The swelling is accompanied by a dull ache. My body is sore, but I'm not sure whether it's from the fall or from yesterday. I grasp my bag, bring it to the front of me, and search through it until I find the water bottle. I twist the lid and tip a little on my bleeding hand. It stings, but the dirt and blood run off my hand and onto the ground.

When the bleeding stops, I twist the cap on the bottle and put it back in the bag, then leverage myself up with my other hand. I wipe my damp face with my arm, take a deep breath, and step to walk again. My ankle throbs, so I limp the rest of the way.

My phone vibrates in my hand, and I swipe a little more dirt off the screen before answering it. "Hello?"

"Where are you?" Elena asks.

"I'm nearly there."

"What's with the heavy breathing? Are you walking?"

"I'll be there soon," I reply and hang up. I turn off my phone, take the SIM card out, then snap the card in half and throw it away.

When I reach the clearing, I can see the silhouette of a person swinging on a swing. I have an inkling it's my sister, and I hobble in her direction. The swing stops abruptly.

"Ava," she calls out and runs toward me.

I close my eyes and brace for the impact. Her arms come around me, and she hugs me fiercely, taking all the air out of my lungs. Everything is painful, especially my ribs.

When she pulls back, she asks, "What's going on?"

"Yeah. What is going on?" a deep voice asks. I jump. The familiar panic makes my stomach churn.

Elena touches my shoulder gently. I try not to flinch, but I can't help it. Every part of me is on edge.

"It's okay," she says, her voice soft. "It's only Jake."

I nod, though my heart doesn't slow.

We are in the shadows, so I can't see her clearly. She grasps my sore hand, and I pull it from hers at once. "I fell over."

"Um . . . okay. Well, let's get you cleaned up?"

I follow the two, who are whispering to each other.

He unlocks a van, and as he opens the door, the inside light comes on. When he gets into it, I get a better glimpse of him. He looks the same as he did at their wedding, though his playful mood from that night is nowhere to be seen.

Elena gasps, one hand covering her mouth, and so many

emotions cross her face. Sadness and anger, then sympathy. It burns me to see that in her eyes. This isn't supposed to be how my life turned out. My shoulders drop. I'm so pathetic.

She wipes the corner of her eye with her hand, but she doesn't speak. She stands rigid and stares at me.

Jake clears his throat. "C'mon, Elena, let's get out of here." When I turn to look at him, his eyes widen, then he looks at his wife and frowns.

"Get in," he says to me, underscoring his words with a jerk of his head.

I avoid eye contact with Elena as I pull the backpack off, get into the back of the van, and slide the door shut.

Her soft cries follow the slam of the car door. His hand goes across to her thigh to comfort her. The guilt of making her cry fills me with regret. I hate seeing her sad because of me.

Once we're driving, Jake's eyes flick between the road and the rearview mirror.

"Do you have anything for her?" Elena asks through sniffling. "Like first aid or a clean towel or something."

"Ah, yeah. There should be a metal box in the back there."

"I'm good," I say.

Elena turns to face me, with her eyes slightly narrowed. "You are far from good." A tinge of frustration weaves into her tone.

"I . . . Thank you for picking me up. I promise I won't stay for long. As soon as I get a job, I'll be out of your hair." Being a burden is my worst nightmare come true.

Her voice softens. "You can stay as long as you like."

"Let me run it through Reaper first before you make promises for a long-term stay—" says Jake.

"I have money. Not much, but I've been saving. I'm happy to help clean and cook and whatever I can until I find a place of my own."

"Since you've asked us to pick you up in the middle of the night. I'm going to presume your husband or ex-husband doesn't know you've left. If we're bringing you into the clubhouse, is he going to come looking for you? What should we expect to happen?"

Focusing on my bag, I fidget with the handle. "He doesn't know I left or where I'm going, so there shouldn't be any issues. He might search for me, but he won't know that I'll be with Elena."

"Yeah . . . and what's with the black eye and bruised cheek?" asks Jake.

"When he lost his job, his drinking got worse, so I packed a bag and started saving money because I didn't know how much longer I could handle his nasty remarks and controlling behavior. But yesterday was the first day that he hit me, and I knew it was time to leave because he was out of control and if I didn't get out now"—I lift my hand to my throat—"I don't know how far he would go next time."

Because there would be a next time . . . There is always a next time.

Elena faces me. "I'm so sorry. Why didn't you leave when it got bad? You should have called me; I would have been there for you."

Worthlessness bubbles up inside of me. "I didn't think it would come to this. We had to get through it together. I really tried to make it work." Self-loathing takes its place because maybe I didn't try hard enough.

Closing my eyes, I bring my feet up onto the seat and pull my knees to my chest to hug myself. Distant chatter continues, and exhaustion weighs heavily on me. I'm floating, followed by music and muffled voices, but the pull to sleep is stronger, and it takes over once more.

TWO
BROKEN INSIDE

Ava

"Don't wake her."

"Why? What if she has a concussion? It's been twelve hours."

My eyes creep open at Elena's voice. The beat of the drums and guitar riffs are coming from the music downstairs. It takes a moment to get my bearings until the memories of last night hit me.

I scan my surroundings. The room is small and plain, with painted white walls and an old wooden chest at the end of the bed, against the wall. I'm in a gigantic bed with faded blue sheets.

"You saw her. She needs all the rest she can get."

I notice the voice. It's Jake. However, his nickname at the wedding was Axle.

"You can come in," I say, my voice hoarse. There's a light thudding in my head.

The door opens slowly, and Elena's head pops around it, a frown on her face.

"Please don't give me the sympathy look," I tell her while she closes the door.

She blows out a breath. "It's not sympathy." She peers at the ground. "I hate seeing you hurting like this."

She sits on the edge of the bed next to me, her eyes traveling around my face. "You know me. I hate conflict, and I'm not one to wish harm on someone but . . ." She blinks furiously, as if trying not to cry.

She's such a gentle soul, and I have no idea how she ended up here, of all places. I put my hand on hers and squeeze.

". . . I hope he gets hit by a bus or something."

I laugh, then flinch. "Don't make me laugh. My ribs hurt."

"What happened to your ribs?"

"I fell awkwardly when he hit me. I wasn't expecting it, but, god, it's painful."

She frowns. "I never imagined him to be violent, but I thought you could have done better."

When I think back to the last couple of years, even before he lost his job, it feels like one hand was around my throat and the other squeezing my heart. Nothing I did was ever good enough.

"I don't want to talk about it right now . . . Anyway, how did you get a biker as a husband? I never got to ask at the wedding." We didn't get to spend much time together, and when I was coming back from the restroom, Beau saw me talking to a biker. That was it. We had to go home.

She gives me a sad smile. "We met through a dating app, and the rest is history. Now, I wouldn't say I belong here"—her eyes dim a little before she keeps going—"but I belong with him."

"I'm happy you found love."

Three loud knocks come from the door. "Lunch is ready."

Elena looks at it. "I won't be long." She then looks at me. "Did you want to come down, or did you want me to get a plate and bring it up for you?"

I pull the sheet up over my chest. "I can't . . ."

"Don't worry. I'll bring it up for you."

"I'm sorry," I say, and it makes me cringe.

"There's no need to apologize," she whispers.

Usually, everything is my fault. "Old habits, I guess."

Her frown deepens. "I'll go get you something to eat."

"Oh, and"—she cringes and looks to the floor—"the bathroom is to the right at the end of the hallway. I put a towel and some clothes on the chest of drawers there." She points to it.

Swallowing thickly, I nod, too choked up to speak.

As she turns the handle and opens the door, she looks at me over her shoulder. "We spoke to Reaper last night and you can stay, but if you could help cook and clean like you said you would, that would be great." She doesn't wait for an answer. She gives me a small smile and closes the door softly.

As I sit up in bed, pain assaults me from different areas. Everything aches. My mind wanders off to Beau. Was he angry when he didn't find me next to him, or would he even care? I grunt. Of course he would care. He would have no one to take his anger out on.

I pull the sheet off myself, but as soon as I stand, stiffness burns my body. When I take my first step, searing pain shoots up from my ankle and my jaw clenches. I hobble over to get the towel, clothes, and my bag and then limp over to the door. My hand rests on the doorknob, and before I open it, I peer down. My jeans have dirt caked at the knees where I fell over, and my coat has a swipe of blood and dirt on it.

I open the door and peek through the crack to see if anyone is around, then step outside and pull it closed behind me. Every step is agony, and I note to ask Elena for painkillers. As soon as I get in the bathroom, I turn the lock and place the towel and clothes on the towel rack.

Sliding my arms out of the coat, I suck in a breath through my teeth. I take my shirt off and undo the button of my jeans and pull them over my hips before stepping out of them. Inspecting my body, I see my palms are red and one has a scab. The side of my body is a mix of blue-and-purple bruises. A large deep purple one is on my hip and another up the side of my ribs. I touch the tender area.

When I look in the mirror, tears stream down my face. I'm a mess. My left eye is red and purple, and my cheek is more of a swirl of purple and blue.

I don't recognize the person in front of me. Bile rises, and I bend over the toilet in time to vomit. With the back of my hand, I wipe my mouth. I take my underwear off and step into the hot water. I cry in the shower because no one can see my tears, my weakness.

Once I'm out and have finished drying myself, knowing that my sister and I are different sizes, I lift the first piece of clothing in curiosity. She should know I wouldn't be able to get my boobs into her shirts and my ass into any pants she owns. I'm relieved that, instead, it's a burgundy dress, and up against me, it looks loose, so it may even fit. As I'm getting changed, a bang on the door startles me.

"What is taking so long? Hurry up, I need to take a piss!"

My breathing quickens, and my heart thrums as I hastily pull the dress over my head and grab my towel and dirty clothes. I open the door and am met by a handsome man. His face morphs from annoyed to curious as he raises a brow and looks me over from head to toe.

"Excuse me," I mutter. I bow my head, waiting for him to move from the doorway.

He remains still, and when I glance up, he's grinning. "Ava, is it?"

My grip on my clothes tightens as I clear my throat, wondering how he knows my name already. "Yes."

"Oh no you don't," Elena says from nearby. She bumps him aside with her hip, allowing me room to move past.

"I was just getting to know her."

I turn, watching their interaction. Elena shakes her head. "No, no, and no."

He winks at me. "Later, Ava."

She groans and follows me into the room. "There's your plate." She signals to the bed. "Sorry it took so long. I was helping to dish out the food, and those guys just didn't stop eating. I'm surprised they aren't fat, to be honest."

"It's okay. I needed a shower anyway."

She tugs at my dirty clothes. "Here, let me wash them."

I pull back. "I can do it."

She pulls them toward her. "Stop being so stubborn. Let me look after you for at least one day."

My shoulders fall, and I reluctantly pass them to her. The side of her mouth lifts victoriously.

"Did you want me to organize a doctor to come and check up on you?"

I'm quick to answer. "No. It looks worse than it is."

Her brow furrows. "Are you sure?"

"It's okay. They are only bruises. They will heal in no time."

"What about getting a protective order? I can ask the club's attorney about it."

I shake my head. "I'm away from him now. That's all that matters."

"I can get Jake to sort him out for you."

"Elena," I warn, "please stop."

She sighs noisily. "Okay . . . I'll wash these for you. I'll be back."

"Just chuck them out."

"What? Why?" She looks at my clothes. "The dirt will come out."

"I want nothing that reminds me of him. Can we go shopping so I can get some clothes?"

Her eyes dart to my bruises. "I'll organize the clothes. You just relax." She forces a smile.

After she leaves, I get up and flick the lock shut, then go over to the window and pull at it to ensure it's locked as well. After finishing the plate of food, I lie down and roll over onto my side. Still feeling drained, I close my eyes and fall back asleep.

THREE
NEW WORLD

Ava

I SIT UP ABRUPTLY, COVERED IN SWEAT. I'M PANTING, TRYING TO catch my breath. The room is dark, but it isn't long until I realize where I am. A blanket of relief covers me. "He's not here," I whisper to myself. I'm on edge and a shadow of who I once was. He's sucked the life right out of me.

The music and voices are loud, reminding me I'm here with more people than just Elena. I will go insane if I stay in this room by myself, dealing with my demons, so I get up and shuffle to the wall before turning on the light. After I blink a few times, my eyes adjust to the brightness. If they are having a party downstairs, it could be the perfect distraction. I grab my makeup bag, unlock the door, and walk over to the bathroom.

After I finish applying my makeup, I lean closer to the mirror. There's no hope of getting rid of the bruises, but I have covered them up somewhat. There's no mistaking my cleavage in this dress. I'm surprised it fits me. I'm lucky it flows out at the bottom. I stare at myself again. This will have to do.

After putting my belongings away, I walk through the hallway. A girl with only a thong on comes running in my direction, so I flatten myself against the wall and look away from her naked body. She's pulling the guy I met this afternoon behind her. He winks at me again as he walks past.

When I reach the top of the stairs, I hesitate. Every ounce of me wants to run back into the bedroom, but I take a deep breath and slowly make my way down. The song playing is "Debonaire" by Dope. I used to love all different music. I'll have to get a new phone to download all my favorite songs, and I'm sure there's new music out I haven't heard yet.

Squeals and high-pitched sounds of laughter make me physically cringe, and when I look over, two women are running away from a man with a different MC cut on. When he catches one, his arm curls around her back, and he pulls her into him and motorboats his face against her boobs. Her head falls back while she laughs.

"Ava!" Elena calls out.

I scan the crowd to see her rushing toward me. My sister is wearing white skinny jeans with a cute blue shirt tied up at the front, exposing her stomach, and it looks as though she's wearing a cut over the top.

When she gets closer, I see that at the top, where a pocket would be, it reads *War Brothers MC*. Underneath it says *Property of Axle*, and it sends shivers up my spine.

"What's this?" I cannot keep the disdain from my voice.

Her brow furrows. "It means that I'm his ol' lady. It's a tradition."

I don't answer, my eyes narrowing a fraction.

She shakes her head. "I can see your mind spinning. It means that I'm off limits to every other man."

"I still don't like it." Not after everything I've been

through. I could wear nothing that suggests I'm the property of a man.

"How are you feeling?"

"A little better after sleep, though I think I could sleep for days."

Her eyes soften and a genuine smile curves on her lips. "That's good."

I look around. "I don't know what I was expecting, but it wasn't this."

MC paraphernalia is plastered everywhere. A flag with their logo hangs on a wall. It's a skull with two guns behind it, with *War Brothers MC* across the top. A motorcycle rests in the wall, and photos of mug shots of the men litter the walls.

Everything is wood and has a masculine style. It has a wooden floor, exposed wooden beams, and wooden furniture, so it has an industrial feel to it. The place is open plan, so I can see what's going on around me.

"It surprised me when I first came here as well." She looks at the bar, then at me. "Do you want a drink?"

I give her a clipped nod and follow her over to where Jake is sitting. When we reach Jake, he puts an arm around her waist. "Ava," he says and tips his beer in greeting.

"Hey, Jake."

Elena sits on the stool next to Jake and pats the spare chair beside her. I take a seat. "Everyone calls each other by their road names, not by their actual names. So Jake's road name is Axle."

"If everyone but you calls him Axle, I'll call him that too."

"Fine by me." She looks at the other guy. "This is Cash. Cash, this is Ava, my sister."

He is tall, wearing a white shirt with his cut over the top, and has short black hair.

"Howdy," he says with a grin as he finishes wiping a glass.

"Nice to meet you, Cash."

"What would you two ladies like to drink?"

"Four shots—all tequilas," I answer, feeling Elena's eyes on me.

He lets out a low whistle. "Big night?"

"Something like that," I mumble, craving the numbness.

As he pours the tequila into four shot glasses, Elena gags. "Ewww. I hate tequila." She peers at me. "Ever since we got drunk off it that time, I haven't been able to touch it."

"Wow, that was a long time ago." I don't remember the taste, but I know it's not pleasant.

Cash places two shots in front of each of us.

"Hmm . . ." Elena looks at the shots like they're poisonous. "It still haunts me."

"I'll have yours, too, if you don't want them."

"No. I'll do it," she grumbles as she picks one up and, with her other hand, blocks her nose. I pick mine up, and we clink glasses and gulp them. The tequila burns the entire way down my throat.

Elena coughs and Axle pats her back. She slides the other shot over to me. "I can't do another." Her face scrunches. "It tastes like what I think nail polish remover would taste like."

Without a second thought, I pick it up and down it, then pick up the other and do the same, not even taking a breath between. It makes my eyes water, and I fight the need to retch, but soon after, a warm sensation fills my stomach. "Two more, please."

Elena gives me a sympathetic smile. "Are you sure?"

I put my hand up. "Yes!" After I slam those drinks down, the stress lifts.

"Why the name War Brothers MC?" I ask.

Her smile slips. "Most of them served in the military. Reaper, Bomber, and Viper were in the military together. When they came back, they wanted that brotherhood again, so they created the War Brothers MC. Bomber's family founded the town, and because Bomber owned this property, the MC decided to set up here, in Crown Village. Jake described it as it gave them a home and a purpose because they got to make friends with other men that went through similar experiences when they were at war."

I respect that, and I raise a brow at her. "So there's more to them that meets the eye?"

"There certainly is," she says as her eyes soften. "Well, I better give you the rundown on everyone here. Jake is the road captain. Cash here," she says and glances at him, "is the treasurer, and as you can see, he's easygoing."

She turns her head to the left and whispers, "The man at the end of the bar with the black hair, that's Bomber." I turn to where she is looking and watch as he slowly brings the glass to his lips and downs his drink, then slams the glass back onto the table.

"He is the sergeant at arms." She leans in closer, making sure only I can hear. "He's very blunt and straight to the point, so don't take it personally."

My eyes widen. "What do you mean by that? I can't handle another man like my husband."

"Oh, no, not like that. I meant he can appear cold, but it's just the way he is. The men here are different to anyone you have met before, but to be clear, none of them hurt women. Well . . . only if they ask for it." Her face flushes pink. "Some women are into that type of stuff."

My head falls back. "Elena. I don't want to know."

"What are you two whispering about?" Axle asks.

Giggling, she looks over her shoulder. "Nothing." She leans in closer again. "So you won't have any issue with Bomber trying to hook up with you, but some others . . ." Before jumping off her chair, she cringes. "I'm going to introduce Ava to everyone," she says to Axle and Cash, then lightly pulls me off my chair.

My head spins from the alcohol, so I grab her arm to stop me from swaying. I'm such a lightweight.

"Make sure you say her name, so they know *exactly who she is*," Axle says.

"I will," Elena replies.

She links her arm with mine, and as we take two steps toward Bomber, a woman steps in front of us and slides in next to him, clutching his arm. When she squeals, I shift to the side to see him grasping her forearm with cold eyes.

"No one touches me," he grates out. It startles me, so I step back and scowl at Elena.

She shakes her head at me. "He won't hurt her, he just"—she looks away before looking back at me and lowering her voice—"he doesn't like them touching him. They keep trying, even though he has made it clear that he won't sleep with them."

"I'm sorry, Bomber, I forgot," the woman says, trying to sound confident, but there's a hitch in her voice. "I can come around later, baby?"

She is so forward. What in the world is this place?

He hisses and lets go of her arm. "No."

It is clear and concise, and no one could have mistaken the edge in his voice. I don't understand why she would try if he didn't even like her touching his arm.

She nods, and when she scrambles out of the way, his eyes land on us. Elena hesitates before giving him a smile. "I wanted to introduce you to my sister, Ava."

His eyes survey my face, and it's a reminder they can see my bruises. He watches me warily and lifts his chin in acknowledgement. I try to smile, though I'm not sure whether it comes across as a grimace.

"Will your husband be giving us any trouble?"

I sharply inhale as my heart beats faster. "I . . . don't think so." He searches my eyes as if trying to find out if I'm telling the truth, and I shift on my feet, my gaze going to the floor. When my eyes reach his again, I reply, "Well, I hope not." He slowly nods at me.

When we turn to leave him, Elena whispers, "I'm sorry. He means well. It's part of his job to ensure the security of the club, so he has to know everything that's going on. He might have more questions to ask you."

My stomach twists, and I don't know whether it's from the alcohol or because I'll be interrogated later.

Elena looks over, searching the room, and points to a chair near the lounge. "The younger one, getting a lap dance with his hat on backward, is Twitch. He's really nice, and he's their computer and all-things-technology expert." He's smiling as he gawks at the woman with the red thong grinding on his crotch.

I look away as I lift my hand to my heated cheek. I'm not used to everyone being so open with their sexuality. "He looks, ah, busy now. Can I meet him later?"

Elena giggles. "Sure." She searches the room once more. "I can't see the prospect around, but his name is Rage."

"Oh, lovely," I reply. Though the alcohol has released some tension, there's still dread from the sound of his name.

Her brow furrows. "It's weird. He's not actually angry in person. I think he gets his name from the fighting competition that the MC hosts. Viper's the one to stay away from. He's the manwhore of the club. Oh, and avoid Demon, too."

"Okay, I'll stay away from them. Demon? The name sounds terrible. What's he look like?" I ask so I can stay far, far away.

"Demon is the enforcer. You can't miss him. He's covered in tattoos and has a mohawk."

At least Beau would never walk into this place with MC men living here.

"Demon's the one that handles club business." She hooks air quotes.

My head tilts to the side. "What do you mean by that?"

"Have you seen the one percent on their cut?"

"Yes, I saw it on Axle's."

"Do you know what it means?"

I answer with a clipped, "no."

"It means they're outlaws. They have their own set of values and laws."

"Okay . . ." I gulp. "But I still don't understand what that has got to do with Demon being a club member."

"So normal people go to jail when convicted of a crime. In the MC, Demon gives out the punishment." She doesn't expand on that, and she doesn't need to.

"Okay, got it. It's a different world here."

"It is," she agrees.

I peek at Bomber again. "Is Demon scarier than Bomber?"

She laughs, and I gawk at her. "It depends on what you think scary is."

"But they won't hurt me?" I ask slower than usual.

She frowns and rubs my shoulder with her other hand. "None of them would hurt you."

"And pretty boy?"

"Pretty boy?" she asks with furrowed brows. "Who's that?" Her eyes widen, and she laughs. "That name suits him. That's Viper, who I was talking about before. Don't be fooled by his panty-dropping smile or smooth talking. He'll try to get into your pants."

"Noted. I saw some woman pulling him along the hallway upstairs."

She rolls her eyes. "That's a normal occurrence for all the men around here. Well, everybody except Jake and Bomber."

After a moment, I laugh inappropriately. "If only Mom and Dad could see us now."

Elena snorts. "It would mortify them. Both of their daughters now being sinners."

"I think I need more alcohol."

She puts my arm around her shoulder, helping me stay upright. "No, you do not. I think it's time for bed."

"What about meeting everyone else?"

"You can do that tomorrow."

"Mmm . . ." I mutter, then yawn, my eyes and body heavy.

Commotion causes our heads to turn to a man with an MC cut on, who is at least six foot five, and a man cowering on the floor below him. "You are no longer welcome here."

The house goes quiet.

The guy on the ground looks terrified, and he furiously nods in response.

"Now, leave." His deep voice echoes in the house. Whoever this man is, he held everyone's attention, and when he spoke, everyone listened.

The other man is shaking. He gets to his feet and runs toward the front of the house.

"I . . . I don't know if I can stay here." My eyes bounce between Bomber and the tall man. When he turns slightly, I can see him side on. He looks somewhat familiar.

"You are safe here with them. They are good men. They're different, but once you get to know them, you will see. Trust me?" Elena asks.

"I trust you."

Four men step forward with a different cut from the others. One of them steps closer to the intimidating man. "I'm sorry, Reaper, that's our new prospect. It won't happen again."

"I don't care who he is. I want him gone, Jude. When our

women say no, they fucking mean it. I have zero tolerance for that bullshit."

"Done." He looks at the men behind him. "It's time to head back to our clubhouse." The men walk out toward the front of the house, but their leader stays behind. "We will set up a meeting soon to talk about the progress and estimated delivery times." The man looks around to everyone and tilts his head forward. "Have a good evening, everyone."

When he leaves, I ask, "Who's that?"

"They were a few members from the Kings of Chaos MC. The last man to leave was their president."

My eyes bounce back to the tall man. "And who is that?"

I'm not yet able to see his full face from where I'm standing.

"Reaper," Elena replies quietly, then pauses. "The president of the War Brothers MC."

He shifts to face our way, and when I see him, it clicks. "Oooh, I saw him at your wedding. I was talking to him there."

I remember how, even in our brief conversation, he made me smile, and it was because he gave me a compliment. My heart squeezes at the thought because it had been so long since I genuinely smiled, and it felt like forever since I had been noticed. Beau and I were together for so long I forgot not all men are the same.

"When Beau and I had sex that night, I was imagining it was Reaper."

She bursts out laughing. "You are drunk."

"Did I say that out loud?"

She giggles again. "Yep." She attempts to help me up the stairs as I lean into her, my arm around her shoulder.

I peek down once more to see Reaper watching me. The intensity startles me and I trip up the last step and land on my ass.

"Are you all right?" Elena's face comes into view, though she's a little blurry.

"Ugh, yeah. I think so."

She grabs my hand and pulls me up. We make it through the hallway, and she opens a bedroom door and helps me through it. I fall on the bed, on my stomach.

"What happened just then with Reaper?" I mumble as my eyes close and exhaustion hits me.

"Even though the women are sweet butts, they are still under the MC's protection."

"Sweet butts," I repeat through a smile. "That's a funny name."

"They do anything the guys need them to, and the MC gives them a roof over their head and food."

One eye cracks open. "So they have to have sex with them?"

"Oh, no," she says with a scrunched-up face. "The women want to. They aren't being forced to do anything, and you can pay your way by helping with cooking and cleaning."

"Thanks, Elena," I mumble. "Thank you for everything."

My eyes open to the twinge of pain of my full bladder. Feeling as though it might burst, I sit up in bed. My hand goes to my head as I groan, knowing I shouldn't have had those shots when I rarely drink alcohol. I stand with a hunched back and walk with one arm low so I don't trip over and one arm held out in front so I don't walk into the wall. My body is still sore, but not as much as it was this morning.

I touch a smooth surface, sliding my fingers across the wall until I grasp the door handle and open it. The music is still on, but it isn't as loud as it was before. A faint light shines from the hallway leading downstairs.

After relieving myself, I throw some water on my face. My hands fall on either side of the sink. This is the reason I don't drink, but I welcomed the few hours of distraction. I think Beau has scarred me forever.

When I reach the bedroom, I open the door, though I swear I left it open. I blame the alcohol. When I walk in, it's as dark as it was before, so I reach out again, trying not to run into anything. When my hands meet the bed, I lie down, and a small moan escapes my lips when I breathe in. Whatever that smell is, it smells so good, and I nuzzle into the pillow and sigh.

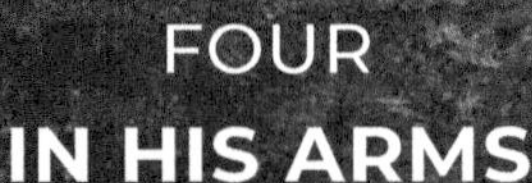

FOUR
IN HIS ARMS

Ava

My body shifts from the heat under me. My hand moves, and my head burrows in, trying to get comfortable, but I'm lying on something hard. There's a distinct, soothing beating sound, *thump, thump, thump*. I open my eyes to a bright light and squint before gazing down. My heart stops. It just stops. I gasp loudly and yank my body off of him and crawl backward. Then I'm falling, and I land on the floor with a thud.

His head turns while his sleepy eyes follow my movements. He blinks a few times as if checking that I'm there, then they widen.

"What are you doing in my bed?" I ask, my voice raised.

He sits up lazily, scratching the back of his head. "You mean, what are *you* doing in *my* bed?" he asks, his voice thick with sleep.

My gaze darts around the room, and the realization makes my stomach sink. "I'm so sorry. I must have mistaken your room for mine last night." A blush burns my cheeks.

"That's the first time I've had a woman apologize for waking up in my bed."

In my head, I'm praying, *Please, God, make me disappear!*

His eyes flick to my cheek, and if it wasn't for his shoulders stiffening ever so slightly, I would have missed that he saw my bruises, but I'm grateful when he says nothing about it.

"Did you know you snore?"

My eyes meet his and narrow. "I do not."

"Yeah, you do. I should know. You slept on top of me for most of the night."

My head falls back with a groan, and I use the edge of the bed to help myself get up. "Well . . ." I say awkwardly. "I'm sorry again." I walk to the door.

"Ava," he says in a deep, husky tone.

I slowly turn to him.

"Did you have a good sleep?" His face is blank, but there's a smugness in his voice.

I nod as my face burns hotter, because last night was the best sleep I've had in a long time, but I won't admit it. Stepping out of his room, I close the door behind me.

"Ava, is that you?"

My body freezes at Elena's voice, and she moves quickly.

Her eyes go wide like saucers. My mouth opens, but I can't speak. She takes my hand and pulls me through the hallway and into a room. Axle is sitting on the edge of the bed, putting his boots on, and looks up at us, watching as we take a seat.

"What happened?" she asks, her voice higher than usual.

I mentally berate myself for even being in this situation. "It's not what you think."

"Well, what was it?"

"I went to the bathroom last night, and I must have accidentally gone into his room instead of mine."

"This ought to be good," Axle says with an ear-to-ear smile. "Whose room did you end up in?"

I gulp and whisper, "Reaper."

Axle laughs, slowly clapping. "Hold up. Hold up." He tilts his head. "He let you sleep in his bed?"

"I didn't have sex with him!" I blurt out. "I'm still married. That's not the type of person I am."

"I know you're not," Elena responds, her voice resonating with understanding. "That's why I was confused when I saw you coming out of his room."

"Hey!" He waves in front of us. "I couldn't care less if you shagged the whole MC."

"Jake!" Elena curses him with narrowed eyes.

He shrugs at her, then gives me his full attention. "Just to be clear, you're telling me you stayed the night in Reaper's bed?"

"Yes," I reply, wondering why he doesn't believe me.

He cocks a brow. "You sure it was Reaper?"

"Seriously?" Elena huffs. "I saw her come out of his room."

"He doesn't let *anyone* sleep or stay in his bed," he says, giving me a pointed look. "He was a sniper in the military. Nothing would get past him. He knew you were there."

I swallow hard, unsure of what to think about that but grateful he let me sleep. Maybe it was how tired I was that I slept so well, or maybe, for once, I unconsciously knew I was safe. The concoction of his scent, warmth, and body was like a sleeping pill I so desperately needed, but I don't need another dangerous man. I've had one. Then why am I attracted to *Reaper?*

THE BRUISES ARE CHANGING COLOR. PARTS ARE A PALE GREEN and yellow. Makeup covers them better now. Even though this morning was one of the most embarrassing moments of my life, today I feel a little different, a little lighter. A new burn of motivation thrums in my veins. Something I haven't felt in a long time.

Elena left a bunch of new clothes in my room, like she said she would. After my shower, I make my way downstairs. The potent smell of alcohol hits me first, and when I look around, Twitch is asleep on the lounge, and the woman with him last night is asleep on the ground next to him. Alcohol cans and bottles litter the floor and nearly every surface I can see.

Footsteps fall behind me. I turn to see a handsome young man. He has a black garbage bag and is picking up the surrounding trash. When he sees me, he gives me an easy smile, so I smile back.

"I'm Ava, Elena's sister."

"The men mentioned you were staying here. I'm Rage."

Elena was right. He does not suit his name.

I peer down at the bag, then gaze around. "Would you like some help?"

His eyes radiate shock. "Hell yeah." His brows pinch together. "I'm starving, though. Can you cook?"

I can't stop the big cheesy smile from taking over my face. "Yes, I can."

He looks to the ceiling and closes his eyes. "Finally," he drawls, "a woman that can cook." He looks back at me. "Can you cook something edible for breakfast for the men?"

My lips mash together as I try not to laugh at "edible." I look to the right and then point to the left. "Is the kitchen that way?" I tilt my head toward the left, guessing it might be through the lounge.

He chuckles and nods. "Yeah, you can't miss it."

I stroll through the house and into the kitchen. Like the

rest of the house, it's dark wood. It contains black stools with worn wooden tops. My hand travels over the counter. It's smooth with a raised surface from the natural wood. The appliances are chrome and state of the art. It has two massive double-door fridges and a coffee machine. I'm in love. There's a buzz of excitement when I see the gigantic oven and cooktop.

"Mornin'," a cheery voice says, making my heart skip a beat. Viper stands a few feet away, making coffee.

I attempt to smile because I want to be polite, but Elena said to stay away from him. "Good morning."

He frowns. "I didn't mean to scare you." He sounds sincere, and it surprises me.

"It's okay."

After the machine finishes adding the coffee to his mug, he adds two teaspoons of sugar. "So what were you smiling at before I bothered you?"

I consider whether to tell him, but I fold. "This." I gesture at my dream kitchen.

He sips and looks at me over the brim of his cup. "The kitchen?"

I sigh. He clearly doesn't get it. "I love cooking. This is a chef's dream."

His lips curve up. "Well, I'm hungry, so go for it."

Excitement returns as I search through the fridges, which are full of food. I pull out the easy things like eggs, sausages, and bacon. Then I move to the oversized pantry, where eight people could easily fit in. My mouth presses into a hard, flat line at the state of the pantry. It's a mess, with pieces of food left on the cupboards. It needs a deep clean. Food containers have been strewn about, so it takes longer than needed, but I grab all the ingredients necessary and put them on the counter. I drum my fingers on the table and turn to Viper.

"Pans?"

"Ahh . . ." He shrugs. "Fuck if I know." He turns to the lounge. "Mercedez, where's the pans?"

There's mumbling, and the one with Twitch stumbles in. Her mascara is smudged underneath her eyes. There are remnants of red lipstick around her lips. She rubs one of her eyes. "What did you say?" she asks in a croaky voice.

"Where are the pans?"

She points. "It's the bottom drawer toward the end."

I lean down and pull the large drawer open and curse at all the kitchen pots and pans carelessly thrown in. There is no order for anything.

"Are you all right?" Viper asks.

"I hate a messy kitchen."

He snorts. "You're going to hate it here, then." He looks at Mercedez and points to the overloaded sink with dirty dishes. "Can you wash up?"

She yawns and moves slowly to the sink.

Another young woman bounces into the kitchen, walks straight to Viper, stands on her toes, gives him a peck on the lips, then turns. "Hi." She smiles, walks to me, and hugs me.

I stand motionless, feeling awkward.

When she pulls back, she says, "I'm Candy. Do you need any help?" I go to answer, but she keeps talking. "I can clean with Mercedez," she offers. She links her hands in front of her. She glances at Viper, then back. "Or I can cook?"

"Can you cook the bacon and sausages, and I'll start on the pancakes?"

"Yes, it's the one thing I can cook," she says, then giggles.

"Did you just say pancakes?"

When I turn, Twitch, Rage, and Viper are standing off to the side with hope in their eyes.

I softly chuckle to myself. "Yes, I did."

Viper rubs his hands together.

"Can you make chocolate chip? My mom used to make them," Rage says longingly.

My heart squeezes. This is why I love cooking. Food makes people happy.

"Sorry, I didn't see any chocolate chips, but I can make both chocolate and vanilla ones."

Viper elbows him. "Stop your whining. I can't even remember the last time we had pancakes."

I move the sausages, bacon, and eggs off to Candy's side and put the hash browns and pancake ingredients on mine, then turn on the gas top.

As I cook, I try to ignore the curious stares and people looking over my shoulder at what I'm cooking until a hand grasps my shoulder. I freeze, then berate myself for acting like that.

When I turn, a woman I haven't met yet is glaring at me. "What do you think you're doing?" she hisses.

My stomach drops. Maybe I should have asked. "I'm . . . helping with breakfast."

Her eyes narrow further as she yanks the spatula out of my hand. "Well, DON'T."

I peek at the stovetop, and I suck in a breath because I don't want to burn the pancakes. Beau hated when I burned the food. I peer back at her, then up at her hand holding the spatula. I snatch it back and pivot. When I flip them over and find the pancakes are a golden color, relief swells in my chest.

"Is this bitch serious?"

I remain with my back to her.

"Do we have a problem here?" I pause at the deep voice resonating around the kitchen, then slowly turn to see Reaper staring between us.

Vera speaks, but Viper talks over her. "Vera is being . . . herself." He pulls a half smile, looking entertained at the current situation.

"Ava is cooking us pancakes," Twitch says, then frowns. "Can't Vera go clean or something? I want my pancakes!"

She doesn't talk back to them, even though her jaw ticks like she wants to.

I already loaded one plate with pancakes, so I extend my arm toward her, encouraging her to grab it. "These are ready. Can you please take them out where everyone is sitting?"

She stares at me before rolling her eyes, grabbing the plate, then walking out of the kitchen. She's followed closely by Viper, Twitch, and Rage.

"Thank you," I say to Reaper, then check on the pancakes.

"The eggs, bacon, and sausages are ready," Candy points out.

"Great." As I open the oven, heat meets my face. With a tea towel, I pull the tray of hash browns out. "These are ready as well."

Elena walks in, smiling at me. "Look at you go." She leans in toward the pancakes and breathes in deeply through her nose, then moans. "I've missed your cooking."

Tears line my eyes, but I blink them away and clear my throat. "Can you help Candy take the food out?"

"I'll be happy to."

I couldn't get the rude woman out of my head, so I bring it up. "There was a woman in here earlier that I hadn't met. She's about my height, chestnut-brown hair. More put together than the other girls."

"I'm guessing you met Vera?"

"That's her. She wasn't happy about me cooking. I thought that's what I was supposed to do. Did I do something wrong?"

She deflates a little. "Sorry, I should have warned you. Most of the sweet butts are manageable, but Vera and Grace are horrible."

"What do you mean by that?"

Her frown deepens, and an unsettling feeling stirs in my stomach. She looks away from me and lets out a heavy sigh. "Nasty women that say nasty things. It's like they never matured past high school."

I monitor her closely. "Are they mean to you?"

Her body stills, and she remains silent.

After I flip over the pancakes, I put my hand on her back. "Is that a yes?"

She turns with a tight smile. "There's a pecking order. I'm an ol' lady, so I am at the top of that. They should respect me. Vera is next because she manages everything in this club-house, not that she does a good job of it, may I add. The other sweet butts come after that."

Her voice doesn't sound convincing, and I hate that she's lying, but I keep my mouth shut because I haven't been open and honest with her, either.

"Have I met Grace yet?"

"She's the one that was talking to Bomber last night."

I turn the stovetop off, rest the final pancake on the plate, and put the dirty pouring cup in the sink. Grasping the plate, I step forward and lower my voice. "What was that about when he grabbed her like that?"

She shrugs. "He doesn't like the sweet butts touching him —or really any woman. The other men have no issues having sex with them, but he's different."

With a tight nod, I follow her through the house to the dining area. The room erupts in cheers and whistles as I bring out the rest of the pancakes, and my cheeks heat as I place it on the small table. A thrill courses through me at their grati-tude, and their appreciation hits me right in the chest, making me smile. Reaper smiles too.

I grab a plate and put a couple of pancakes on it with some cut-up strawberries and a little cream. Everyone is sitting around a humongous wooden table. Elena has a spare seat next to her, though the man with all the tattoos is sitting on the other side of it. My feet remain glued to the ground as I stare at Demon, but when Elena makes eye contact with me and waves me over, I have no choice but to go take a seat.

When I reach them, Axle smiles at me. "So good," he says through a mouthful of food.

"I'm glad you like it," I say as I place my plate on the table. When I take a seat, I shuffle my chair closer to Elena.

"Like it? I love it! Elena can't cook for shit."

I try not to laugh, but I fail miserably. Elena swats him with her hand. "Hey, I try."

"Yes, babe," he says, smiling lovingly at her.

They are the cutest, and I'm so happy for them.

As I eat my pancakes, I feel Demon's eyes on me. I wipe the corners of my mouth, hoping I don't have food all over my face. I peek up under my lashes, and I was right—he is staring. I find it strange. He wasn't checking me out and it wasn't a hostile glare, but I'm not sure what it was and I don't want to be rude, so I turn my body toward him. "Hi, I'm Ava."

A wicked smile slides over his lips, and he stares at me without responding. My breathing hitches. I shuffle in my seat, suddenly feeling the heat on my cheeks again. His eyes study me, both intense and curious. "So I heard . . ." He tilts his head. "I'd introduce myself but . . ." He lifts his hand to my face but doesn't touch me. "I'll take a guess from your hesitation to sit next to me. You already know who I am."

Swallowing hard, I give him a sharp nod. I've met no one like him before.

He relaxes further into his chair with his crooked smile and pops a strawberry into his mouth, looking at the others around the table.

Elena clears her throat, and when I lift my gaze, she mouths *sorry*.

I focus on finishing my food, but I'm a little confused about my interaction with Demon. At least he didn't ask me about my husband or what I'm going through. In the short period I've been here, I've noticed that they don't pretend to be anyone other than who they are, and even if what they do or say is shocking, it's refreshing because Beau was fake and a different person with me than what he was with others.

"How long are you staying?"

I turn to the left to see Bomber's eyes on me. Everyone's voices stop, and my heart speeds up. I'm taken aback. "I'm not sure yet . . . I was hoping to do up a résumé and start applying for jobs."

"No!" Twitch and Viper say simultaneously.

My eyes go wide.

"She stays with us. We need food," Viper says, looking at Reaper. "Can we make an exception for Ava and pay her? No one else can cook around here." Then he gives the women around the table a cheeky half smile. "No offense, ladies."

His charm impresses me.

Elena tuts. "If you need any help with your resume or looking for jobs, let me know."

Axle shakes his head at me from behind her, and I try to hide the smile on my face. "Thanks, I appreciate it."

"You should have asked Ava before announcing it across the dinner table," Reaper responds, his eyes flicking between us.

Elena's phone rings, distracting me from the rest of their conversation. Axle groans. "Why won't you answer it? It's been ringing all morning."

She bites her lip and glances at me. Tension takes hold of my shoulders. "I don't want to," she replies with a bite in her tone.

Axle's eyes narrow. "If you don't answer it, I will."

She grasps her phone and walks away, so I follow her.

"Hello. Yes, it's Elena. Yes, I heard she's missing."

My stomach drops at her words. We bypass the kitchen and go out the back door.

"I don't know. I haven't seen her."

She paces and groans. "I don't know what you want me to say. I said I haven't seen her. Okay, I'll be in touch with you if I do. Bye."

She turns to see me and jolts back, grasping her chest.

"Who was that?" I ask cautiously.

She lets out a long sigh as she bows her head. "Beau reported you missing." She looks up at me with sympathy in her eyes. "The police were asking about you."

With a lump in my throat, all I can do is nod in acknowledgment.

She reaches out and puts her hand on my arm. "Beau and our parents have called as well. I should have told you, but I didn't want to upset or worry you."

"What did Beau say?" I hate that my fear of him makes my voice unsteady.

"The same as our parents. Asking if I have spoken to or seen you. Mom and Dad sounded worried. Beau also sounded worried. It's scary how convincing he sounds."

I let out a chuckle that has no humor in it. "He used to belittle me and threaten me, but when we went out to dinner or to our parents' house, he was a different person. He's very charming, but with me, he could change like that." I snap my fingers.

"The officer mentioned that if you were to contact them to say you were okay, for whatever reason you left, they don't have to disclose your whereabouts to anyone. I gather that includes Beau."

Her words cut through me like a blade, and I feel no comfort because there's always the "but what if Beau finds out?"

I shake my head abruptly. "I'm not ready."

She gives me a small smile. "I understand. In the meantime, I'll ask Axle to talk to the club's attorney to make sure it's legit."

After helping to clean up after breakfast, Elena and Axle go off by themselves. I'm left alone, a little lost without Elena. Two women don't like me, and the rest seem to have no interest in making new friends.

"Thank you for breakfast," Reaper says from behind me.

I turn to him and grin at his praise. "That's okay. I enjoy cooking, and your kitchen is amazing."

His brows lift high in surprise. "I didn't know a kitchen could make a woman happy."

"Well, it surely can."

"You're an easy woman to please."

"I've always dreamed about working in a beautiful kitchen like yours, with all new state-of-the-art cooking equipment. The black color mixed with the natural wood and the stone countertop is a stunning combination."

"If you like it so much, I can bring the suggestion of you cooking for the MC to church for a vote?"

"I'd be happy to cook for all of you," I reply, hoping I can.

I've been out of work for so long that I have no computer to do a résumé and I can't afford to spend money on it, so cooking while I'm here is my only good option. Luckily for me, I love cooking.

FIVE

FIGHTING FOR AIR

Ava

I GO BACK INTO MY ROOM, AND IT ISN'T LONG UNTIL MY ANXIETY returns. I wish I was back in Reaper's bed so my mind would stop torturing me with thoughts of Beau finding me and taking me back to hell. I wonder if he would physically hurt me to teach me a lesson or tell me he will never hurt me again but mentally torture me instead, like he has been for years. *Ava, your dress is too short. You look like a prostitute. Have you gained weight? What have you been doing all day? Why do you always forget something when you buy groceries? Are you dumb or do you enjoy pissing me off?*

My nerves coil up so tight I slam my fist against the bed, hating that even though he's not here, he still has control over me, making me scared and vulnerable.

The thought of leaving the MC because Beau causes too much trouble has my stomach churning. Bomber has made it clear that he doesn't want me bringing any drama into the club. It scares me that I may have to leave, but I understand why. They don't owe me anything.

Knock, knock, knock. The door handle wiggles.

"Please, Ava, let me in. You've been in there for a while."

I sniffle, my nose still blocked from crying. "I'm good."

"Then unlock the door."

"I need some time to myself, Elena." My voice breaks a little at the end.

"Okay," she says, defeated. "I'm always here if you need me."

"I know."

Brief silence falls, then she speaks. "You have one day, or I swear I will break the lock."

A sliver of lightness fills my chest at her attempt to be stern with me. "Okay, I promise."

I roll over into the fetal position, pulling the duvet up to my chest. The sadness and stress are overwhelming. I don't have the strength to get out of bed, and I want no one to see me like this. I'm mentally drained, as all the what-ifs and worst-case scenarios keep manifesting, and with each thought, it's like another punch to my already-worsening mental state.

Over the afternoon and night, Elena keeps checking in on me and leaving food, but I can't eat, not with the stress. I try to sleep, but I can't, and I lie there, awake, with my eyes closed.

Needing to go to the bathroom, I pop my head out the door. It must be late because the music has died down again and no one is in the hall, so I drag my feet to the bathroom.

Once I'm done, I open the door but jump backward when I see Reaper leaning against the wall, staring at me.

"At church, the men agreed that you'll cook for us and we'll pay you a wage." His eyes search my face. I'm sure I look as terrible as I feel.

"Thank you," I breathe out. At least I have a job now. "I'll be up early tomorrow to cook for everyone."

"Are you going to tell me why you locked yourself in the room all day?" His voice is tinged with curiosity.

"I don't want Beau to find me." My eyes widen at my honesty.

"What makes you think he will?"

I shrug. "Bad habit of always assuming the worst." Yes, I was paranoid, but if experience taught me anything, it was that Beau always got his way.

"Do you know how to shoot a gun?"

"No."

"I'll teach you tomorrow after breakfast."

"There's no need, really. But thanks."

He raises a brow. "A woman needs to know how to protect herself."

I don't answer because there's truth to what he's saying.

"I can tell you that you're safe living under the roof of my MC, but it's important to learn how to protect yourself in case you ever need to. At some stage your husband will come looking for you, so you should be prepared for anything."

"Why are you letting me stay here then?"

His eyes soften. "If he hit you before, he will rain down hell on you if you return."

The truth makes me flinch.

"Now, get some sleep. I want a bacon and egg burger for breakfast."

My alarm rings, so I grab my phone and turn it off. Today, I woke up with a purpose. Even though it's to cook, it's something I love to do, and at least I can save more money.

After getting changed into jeans and a fitted T-shirt, I grab my wallet, and move down to the kitchen. I gasp when I arrive and see dirty pans in the sink, the overflowing bin, and cups and beer bottles sitting on the kitchen counter. From last time, I should've known that they wouldn't have cleaned up.

When I search the fridges, only a little bacon is left, and ten eggs. In the pantry, I can't find any bread. Dread slithers through me.

"Okay, think," I mumble to myself.

"What about?"

I let out a small scream. "I didn't see you come in."

Rage gives me a half smile and wipes his forehead with his forearm. "Yeah, sorry, I should be more careful around you because . . ." His eyes dart away as he stands awkwardly. "Everything you have been through and all."

Viper comes up behind him, breathing heavily. "You *are* fast."

They are both shirtless, so I gather they have been out exercising. It's impossible not to notice their very fit, very muscled bodies.

When Viper sees me, he flashes one of his cocky smiles. "Hey, darl."

My lips tighten. I don't know how to act around Viper because Elena said to stay away from him.

Rage chuckles and looks to Viper. "I've never seen a woman look at you like that."

Viper playfully whacks his shoulder. "I don't like it." Viper's eyes soften when he glances at me with his hands up in defense. "I don't want to scare you. If you're worried I'll come on to you, then I give you my word that I won't."

I give him an appreciative smile. "Good. Thank you. Now,

I don't want to wake Elena and Axle, so could you take me to do some shopping for breakfast?"

His eyes brighten at the mention of food. "Sure. When did you want to go?"

I bite my bottom lip, hating to sound needy. "Now . . . if that's okay? I didn't want everyone to wait too long to eat."

He looks down at his attire, which is only a pair of shorts. Sweat shimmers across his chest. "I won't be long. I'll go have a shower and get changed."

With Viper's and Rage's muscles and model-like faces, I can see their appeal, but it's the rugged, solid masculine men that are more attractive . . . like Reaper. I shake my head to rid myself of those thoughts.

After Viper leaves, I search the drawers until I find a garbage bag, and then I pick up the bottles and trash. Rage does the same. From the kitchen, we move through the house. By the time we reach the front of the house, we have two full large bags.

Rage's smile spreads. "Thanks for helping."

I smile back. "That's okay. Why doesn't anyone help you?"

"I'm a prospect. It's my job."

"What about the women?"

He chuckles like the question is ridiculous, then cocks a brow. "Because they're lazy. I kept asking them to help at the beginning, but I soon learned that it's easier to do it myself than nag at them." He sounds like a single mother dealing with children.

Footsteps thud, and I look over to see Viper hurrying down the stairs and approaching us. He opens a drawer from a table near the front door and pulls out keys.

I peer back at Rage. "Can you wash up in the kitchen for me so I can start cooking straight away when I get back?"

"Sure. I'll have a shower and get onto it."

When I step outside, I follow Viper down the stairs. I stop, then turn to eye the front of the clubhouse. It reminds me of a small castle with the roof and sandstone cladding. The land around the house is clear, but further along, near where the forest begins, is a fence.

When I turn back, I dash toward Viper. My heart pounds as we walk to a large shed and a few cars and a row of motor-cycles. He moves to the truck and gets in. I have to use the side rail to help lever myself up into the truck because it is high.

The truck starts, and we move along the dirt road surrounded by trees and shrubs. *He's a friend of Elena's and Axle's, so I'll be okay*, I repeat in my head. It feels foreign being in a car with another man, even if only to go to the store.

I peer out the window as we drive along further. I'm surprised at how peaceful it is out here. We bypass a large warehouse next. "What's that used for?"

"We hold fighting matches."

"Is that where Rage fights?"

"He sure does. That kid has talent for his age."

"Kid? How old are you?"

He glances at me. "I'm in my late twenties."

I snort. "You are younger than me."

"Not that much older," he says in a flirty tone.

"How do you know how old I am?"

"Axle."

Damn, Axle!

We eventually reach the asphalt road, where he looks right and left before continuing. Ten minutes later, we reach the small town of older and newer buildings. He turns into a parking lot and parks the truck off to the side of a shopping complex. A distant bark echoes from a small old cottage next to the complex. A dilapidated kennel has a rottweiler tied to it. A part of the dog resonates with me.

Viper clears his throat.

I peek back at him, and he shakes his head. "I'm not getting my ass kicked because you wanted to pat a dog and got bitten." He points to the complex. "Now, let's go get food so we can go home. I'm hungry, woman."

I exhale and nod, following him. He pushes the cart while I take the food off the shelves and place it inside. I would usually scan the items for the cheapest available, but I don't bother because if it's cheap, the men may not like it. Plus, my mind keeps drifting back to the dog.

As we go through the aisles, Viper gives a seductive smile to a few women who pass us by. They stop and talk to him, so I take over the cart and keep moving along, not interested in listening to their conversation.

Viper jogs up to me at the checkout and assists with placing the last bags into the trolley. "You're quick. One minute you're there and the next you're gone."

"We have frozen food in the cart. I didn't want it to defrost." That wasn't the only reason, but I decide against mentioning anything else.

"That's $402.05. Will that be cash or card?" the cashier asks.

"Cash," I reply and pull out my purse.

Viper snorts and puts his arm across me, giving the cashier $100 notes. She giggles and says, "Thank you, Viper." He smiles at her as she gives him the change, and she blushes profusely.

I push the cart along to the truck. We place the groceries in the back.

"I'll push the cart back into the bay," I tell him, since it's closer to the dog. The dog watches me and barks once, but as I get closer, its tail is wagging.

"Ava!" Viper yells out with warning in his tone, but it only makes me fasten my pace.

The dog's tail speeds up, *wap, wap, wap*. My heart beats faster as I approach, but when it reaches me, it sniffs my hand, my shoes, and around my legs, then leans into me, so I pat its head. The dog's coat is smooth, but when I glance at my hand, it's dirty.

"Where's your water?"

He licks my hand, lapping up the attention.

There's a red bucket tipped on its side.

Heavy footsteps approach, and I hesitantly turn to see Viper. He runs his hand through his hair. "Ava! What were you thinking?"

I wasn't thinking. I watch the dog, who's frozen, his tail no longer wagging. "I'd step back if I were you." His eyes go wide, and he jumps back, out of reach of the dog.

"Can you get some water? The dog doesn't have any."

He groans. "Only if we go home afterward because your sister and Reaper will skin me alive if you get hurt."

Why would Reaper care? I think to myself. I frown at the dog, and he looks up at me with his big, sad, brown eyes.

"Don't even think about it," Viper clips.

"But he's dirty, and he's got no water. The owners obviously don't care about him."

Viper's jaw drops. "You seriously want to steal a dog right now? Just because I wear this"—he gestures to his MC cut—"it doesn't mean I'm a criminal." He smirks but turns serious. "And anyway . . . it looks like it wants to bite me."

I laugh but stop once I hear a voice.

"What are you doing?" a man asks. I turn to see a man wearing a dirty white tank top and small shorts approaching us.

Viper rushes to step in front of me with no sense of safety for himself. I suck in a breath, but the dog doesn't go for him. Instead, his eyes are trained on his owner. A deep growl resonates from next to us.

"What's going on here?" the man asks.

I step to the side, but Viper moves with me, blocking my view. "We are leaving now," he says.

But I move again. "Hi."

Viper hisses at me.

"We were appreciating the beauty of your dog. My friend here," I say as I glance at Viper, who's giving me the death stare, "was just going to get water to fill his bucket."

The man squints, but the dog's growl gets louder, his curled lip baring his teeth.

"You were getting water for this mutt? Stupid thing—he's always barking. Keeps me awake."

I wince. "If the dog is too much trouble, I can take him off your hands for you."

"For fuck's sake," Viper says under his breath.

The man scratches his chin. "It will cost you. I was going to use it for dogfighting, but I'd have to sedate it just to get near it."

From the moment I saw the dog, I had a gut feeling. My instincts were right. It is meant to be.

"How much?"

Viper shakes his head. "That dog ain't going to the clubhouse until you ask Reaper."

"Sure," I reply with my hand out, waiting for him to give me his phone.

Viper raises his brow, then gets his phone out of his pocket, presses a few buttons, and hands it to me.

A deep voice comes through. "Reaper."

"Hi, Reaper, it's me, Ava."

"What are doing on Viper's phone?"

My eyes widen at the first thing out of his mouth. "He took me to get groceries."

No reply.

"Are you there?"

There's a heavy breath. "Yes."

"Well . . . you know how you wanted to teach me how to protect myself."

Viper cocks his head to the side while Reaper answers. "Yes. Where is this going?"

I swallow the lump in my throat. "I had another idea."

"Hmm . . . and what's that?" Amusement tinges his voice.

"Can I bring a dog back to the clubhouse? Please? I'll look after him," I blurt. "He won't get in the way, and I'll take the dog with me when I leave."

If it were anything else, it would horrify me to beg a man to let me have something, but this dog is different. I've wanted him more than anything else in a long time.

Viper stifles a laugh. "Yeah right. The dog might bite someone, though."

I narrow my eyes, warning him to be quiet.

"And how big is this dog?" Reaper asks.

Viper's lips lift into a blinding smile, so I know he heard. He leans down, closer to the phone. "It's a damn rottweiler. The thing's massive."

Reaper chuckles. "Will it make you feel safe?"

"Yes," I reply sharply.

"On one condition."

"And what's that?" I reluctantly ask.

"Only if you learn how to use a gun."

My heart beats faster. "Yes, that won't be a problem." My voice heightens in excitement.

"Okay, well, I'll see you when you get back."

"Thank you, thank you," I reply and hand the phone to Viper, then smile up at the man. "I'll take him."

SIX

BUILDING RELATIONSHIPS

Ava

WE ARE SITTING ON THE LOUNGE WHEN ELENA SAYS, "I can't believe you got a dog."

"His name is Conan."

"That is not a dog's name."

Lifting my chin, I say, "It is so." I lean down, patting Conan, who's lying by my feet. "I thought you loved animals."

She shuffles closer to Axle. "Not ones that are going to eat me."

"He seems fine with women. It's men he's wary of, but he has showed no sign of aggression to anyone since I brought him here. He's just been following me around, but I get the impression if he senses aggression or a threat, it might be a different story."

"Remind me never to yell, and it's not a dog, either," Axle says. "It's a small horse."

I peer back to Conan. "Don't you listen to them," I coo.

"It's one dog. Did he really need all that stuff? I saw the truck when you arrived. It was packed."

I arch a brow in disbelief. "He's a big dog, and it's not like the MC had anything for him."

Axle snorts. "You bought the dog clothes!"

Without a beat, I correct Axle. "His name is Conan." I can't help but smirk. "You never know—it might get cold."

"Poor dog," he replies under his breath.

"It's good to see you smile."

I purse my lips at Elena's comment. Then Conan looks up at me, so I pat him. "I always wanted a dog. I wanted the company . . . and the affection, but Beau said no."

"Why didn't you just get one anyway?" Axle asks.

If only it were that easy. I shake my head. "You don't understand."

"What don't we understand?" Elena asks.

I peek up at her but pause, unsure whether I want to bring it up. "Well, first, I didn't have access to the bank account. He only gave me cash to pay for groceries. I didn't work, so I had no money. When his drinking got worse, I spent less on groceries and put some money aside in case I needed it."

I looked down at Conan. "We only had one car, and I could only drive it when Beau said I could, and I don't know for sure, but I'm pretty sure he had a GPS tracker on the car. He seemed to always know where I was and where I went. I tried not to think too much about it, to ignore his controlling behaviors, but I reached my limit. I asked for a dog once. He said no, and when he said no, it meant no, and if I got the dog, he would have yelled at me and would have given the dog away." *Or killed it.*

"I hope he comes looking for you," Axle says. "I want to punch him for you."

"Are you ready?" a deep voice asks, which makes me

recoil. I glance up to see it's Reaper. Conan stands and turns, his eyes trained on him.

"He's a good guard dog."

It makes me smile. "He is."

"Are you ready to use a gun?"

My hands fidget in front of me. I know I promised, but I'm still dreading it.

"Axle taught me," Elena says. "Trust me, you will be fine."

Conan and I follow Reaper through the house. I can feel the others staring as we walk through, and when I glance up, Vera and Grace are watching me through narrowed eyes. As we pass the kitchen, I bend and grab the bag of dog food and continue until we're outside.

"Wait a moment," I call out to Reaper as I walk over to Conan's bowl and fill it.

Reaper's patiently waiting as I hurry back to him. He's wearing black jeans that cover his tree-trunk legs and a fitted black shirt that stretches over his chest, with his cut over the top. His height, solid build, and deep voice epitomize a masculine man.

When I reach him, we walk along a gravel road. I have to rush to catch up to his long strides.

"Thanks for letting me have the dog here."

"Viper said you went straight up to the dog. What made you think it wouldn't bite you?"

I think back. "His tail was wagging, and he had a doggy smile."

Reaper shakes his head. "You trust too easily with appearances. Not everyone wants to be your friend."

I frown. "I'm not naive."

He releases a throaty chuckle. "I never said you were, but you shouldn't have put yourself in a dangerous situation like that."

He's probably right, but in that circumstance, I made the right choice.

We walk for ten minutes until three thick wooden planks with white-and-red bull's-eyes on them are ahead of us. He pulls a small gun from his holster. "The gun is not loaded, but safety is paramount." He holds the gun and points his index finger along it. "You don't point the gun at anyone unless you plan to shoot it. Otherwise, keep it aimed at the ground. Your finger should be straight against the frame of the gun."

I swallow thickly, as if trying to swallow my nerves, but it doesn't work.

"When you grip the gun, your hand needs to be high and your grip needs to be firm."

"I don't think I can do this."

"Yes, you can. Today we'll focus on grip and stance, and when you're comfortable, you can practice firing the gun at the target."

"Okay," I say through a long exhale. "I can do that."

He hands me the gun and puts his hand over mine. His touch sends a subtle shiver up my spine. "You need to grip the gun tighter." I do, and he bends and taps my thigh. "Spread your legs shoulder-width apart and bend your knees slightly." Embarrassment and *something else* I haven't felt in a long time flood me, making my skin heat, but I try my best to ignore it and follow his instructions. His eyes scan my stance, then he stands next to me. "Now, face your target and lean forward, with arms straight out."

When my arms come out, I feel his criticizing eyes on me.

"Perfect."

His praise hits me in the chest, but I bite back a grin.

"Now, put your finger on the trigger and remember the gun isn't loaded."

I release a shaky breath and move my index finger to the trigger.

"Pull back slowly. Do you feel that wall?"

"Yes."

"Watch the front sight and squeeze the trigger back."

A light crack snaps when I pull my finger back, and the gun moves.

I drop my arms, and with one hand, I pass it back to him. "I really don't like it, and I'm shaking, so I don't think I'll be good at hitting any target."

He gives me a reassuring smile. "I know it's daunting, but you did well. It takes time and practice to get used to it."

I learned something different, and I appreciate he's trying to help me.

We walk in the direction of the clubhouse. "How did you sleep last night?"

My shoulders drop. "Not good. I'm tired today."

"I didn't sleep well, either."

My eyes dart to the ground. We had a better night's sleep when we were in the same bed *together*.

"What are you going to get up to now?"

"I think I'm going to introduce Conan to his toys."

He gives me a small smile, though it looks like he's trying not to laugh at me.

"What?" I ask defensively, with a hint of amusement.

"Nothing." He's quick to respond. "I've got to talk to Viper first. I'll be back." He walks toward the people sitting on the seats.

When I reach the house, Conan is inside his new doghouse. It was worth every cent to see him happy. He gets up to greet me.

"Hold on," I tell him, then go inside and head to the cupboard where I store his things and pull out a squeaky, soft chicken toy and a tennis ball and make my way out the back.

As soon as I open the door, Conan's tail rises and wags.

His awkward jump of excitement makes me laugh. He pounces up on me next, making me step back.

"Wow! Conan," I say as I budge him with my arm, "get down before you push me over."

He drops, though his tail is in full force. I place the toy on the roof of his dog kennel and bend, showing him the ball. "Look what I have." He sniffs it and licks my hand. "Are you ready?" I pull my arm back and fling the ball as far as I can. His eyes follow the ball and he sprints after it.

I skim the clubhouse and see Reaper watching me as Vera, Candy, and Viper talk around him. He gives Viper a chin lift, then walks toward me. Vera's eyes narrow.

Conan comes running back and drops the ball at my feet. When I pick it up, it's wet and thick with slobber. I grimace. "Conan, gross!"

A throaty chuckle comes from beside me as I throw the ball again. Reaper looks amused, though I feel Vera's hostility boring holes into my back.

"Are you with Vera?" He inches back with a quizzical look on his face. I nudge my head in her direction. "She does not look happy."

He turns back, and Vera's eyes soften. Then she goes back to talking to Viper and Candy.

"There's nothing between us, and there never will be. I've told her many times."

I give him a tight smile, thinking she has not gotten the hint, and if she didn't hate me before, she does now.

Once everyone goes inside and Conan is exhausted, I walk inside to Axle, who's sitting by himself in the lounge. "Where's Elena?"

He turns his head from the TV. "She said she was going to the bathroom."

Knowing I need to wash my hands after spending time

with Conan, I walk in the bathroom but pause when I hear Grace's voice.

"And you call yourself an ol' lady." Laughter erupts.

When I peek around, I see it's Grace standing in front of Elena. Her back is against the wall and her head is bowed. It makes the hairs on the back of my neck stand. I notice the signs. The taunting and ridicule are something I know all too well, and the sudden onslaught of anger burns through me.

I rush to them. "Leave her alone."

All heads turn to me. Elena's eyes go wide while Grace laughs. "What are you going to do about it?"

My hands clench by my sides.

Grace steps close to me, her eyes studying me, and she smiles. "You don't scare me. You're pathetic, having a cry because your husband hurt you." She huffs. "Most of us women have gone through so much worse. You two are weak. You both don't belong here."

Elena steps around her and strides over to me. "Don't worry about her," she whispers. "She's not worth it." She pulls me by my hand, and we walk away from her.

"Is she always like that toward you?"

Elena smiles but knits her brows at me. "When none of the men are around."

"Tell Axle."

"It will only make it worse."

"How will it? Axle will put them in their place."

"Vera is with Reaper, and Vera and Grace are best friends, so I've always been reluctant. I didn't want to put Axle in a difficult position."

My stomach plummets. "Reaper *is* with her . . . He told me he wasn't." I can't hide the disappointment in my voice, but it explains why she was not happy.

"They aren't a couple, but they have sex." Her face scrunches. "I think she wants to be his ol' lady."

"Why would Reaper let me sleep in his bed, then?"

A smile tugs on the side of her lips. "He's not into her."

"What about Grace? What's her deal?"

"She used to sleep with Axle before he met me. So, in her head, I took her man."

I huff as my anger sizzles. "If either of them starts on you again, come and tell me. I'll always be by your side when you need me."

She smiles and playfully barges into my shoulder. "It's okay. I'll be fine. I ignore them."

She turns when I stop. "I'm serious. I haven't felt anger like that in a long time. I won't let anyone bully my little sister."

"Okay, okay." She chuckles. "I'm not so little anymore."

I smile back. "You will always be my little sister."

The men walk past us and into a room with a door I've paid little attention to. The wooden door displays a carving of the War Brothers MC logo. When Axle reaches us, he leans over and presses a kiss to Elena's cheek. "We've got church."

Now, I know little about MC clubs, but I know what church means. "I'm guessing club business?" I ask Elena.

"Yep."

"I'd better get a start on lunch, then."

Her hand comes out toward me. "I'd wait. Sometimes after church, they leave to do whatever they do."

"You don't know?"

"No . . ." She pauses. "And I don't think I want to."

Viper said he wasn't a criminal, but they are bikers, so he probably lied.

I step closer to the window and gaze at the cloudless sky, so I turn to Elena. "Is there a path or somewhere we can go for a walk? It's nice weather, and I don't want to sit around all day. I'm sure Conan will love it, too."

She looks away, as if in thought. A hand comes to her chin.

"There is, actually. The MC has a small cabin up the mountain. There's a road that leads there. At a guess, I would say it would be an hour's walk."

"Great. I'll go get my shoes on, and I'll meet you back here."

She nods. "I'll wait for Axle to see what they're doing. My trainers are by the front door anyway."

I move up the stairs and through the hallway and open my bedroom door to see my bag open. My heart hammers. I dart over to it and fumble through it, pulling out clothes and toiletries and my birth certificate. When I reach my wallet, I pull it out and unzip it and count the notes.

A rush of relief hits me when all the money is there. The lack of sleep is taking a toll on me. Maybe I left it open and I don't remember doing it. I put all the items back in, bend down, then slide the bag under the bed. I grab my shoes, sit on the bed, and put them on, tying my shoelaces as I go.

When I reach the top of the stairs, I can see the men coming out of the room they were in. As I step down, my pace slows as I sense the tension in the room. There are no laughs or smiles. All have stern looks on their faces.

"Be safe," Elena says to Axle, then wraps her arms around his neck.

His arms come around her waist. "You have nothing to worry about, babe."

She gives him a chaste kiss on the lips, then drops her arms.

"We won't be long. We should be back later tonight. Rage and Twitch will stay with you two. If you have any problems, I'm a phone call away."

He kisses her once more. Her body slouches as she watches him leave.

When I reach the bottom, I walk toward her. "Are you okay?"

She sighs. "Every time he leaves, I feel sick to my stomach, and I don't get any relief until he returns."

"I'm sorry," I reply, not sure of what to say because I don't know what they are doing and how dangerous it might be. "How about we go for that walk so we can get away from the other women?"

She pauses. "Okay, you get Conan and I'll let Twitch know."

I walk through the house and out the back door. My body stiffens when I can't see Conan. Maybe I should have put him on a leash. "Conan," I yell and walk farther out, searching around the table and chairs, then around the bonfire. "Conan!" I shake my head at my stupidity. He most likely doesn't recognize his name yet.

Loud motorcycles pierce the air, making me jolt. Through it, I can faintly hear barking. He must be out the front. The loud rumbling seems to get farther away as I walk through the house, and when I push the door open, I can see the last few motorcycles tear down the road, kicking up a cloud of dirt in the air as they go.

Conan is standing next to Elena, watching the motorcycles.

She turns. "I was just coming to get you to tell you Conan is here."

"It's fine."

Conan turns at the sound of my voice and walks over to me with his long tongue hanging out of his mouth.

"Are you ready to go for a walk?" I ask enthusiastically.

His tail wags faster, and I bend down to pat his head.

"Twitch gave me a walkie-talkie," she says as she clips it onto her belt. "The service here can be unpredictable."

We follow the dirt road, but instead of going straight ahead, we veer left. The road has a rocky surface and ditches.

High shrubs grow on both sides, and plants grow along the hump between the tire tracks.

A ringing filters through the air. Elena stops, puts her hand in her pocket, and brings her phone up to her face. She groans when she sees who's calling but answers it anyway. "Hi, Mom."

I swallow thickly. Mom's muffled voice booms through the phone, but I can't make out what she's saying.

"I still haven't heard from her, either," Elena says as she looks at me. "No, I'm not lying. I'm sure she's safe." She pauses. "Okay, I'll let you know if she calls. Bye."

I glance at Conan, who is ahead of us, sniffing around a tree.

"We spoke to the club's attorney. She said the police were telling the truth. You can call them and say you're safe, and you don't have to tell them where you are."

My chest constricts. "I don't think I can do that yet."

"It will call off the search party, and Mom and Dad will know that you're okay."

"Beau won't stop looking for me." Tears threaten to fall. "I can't go back to him." My voice is strained.

"Even if he finds you, he can't force you to go anywhere."

I shake my head. "You don't know what he's capable of. He will say and do anything to get his way. He must be in control of the situation and of me."

I search for Conan because he's no longer in front of us. "Conan!" I call out. Off to the left, I see his tail. He comes out from the bushes and jogs on the path again. The hill gets steeper, making my breathing heavier.

"What did you mean by being in control?"

"Everything. He controlled the money. I never got a say about sex. It was always when and what he wanted, regardless of whether I wanted it or not." A shiver creeps down my spine at the memories. "I was told it was my duty to please him, and if I didn't, he would go elsewhere." My vision blurs with fresh tears. "I wanted to become a chef, but he wanted me to stay home and be a housewife because he wanted kids."

I wipe my eyes with my hands and chuckle. "We kept trying for kids, but it never happened for us. When we went to the doctor and had tests, I was diagnosed with endometriosis."

Elena's arms come around me, squeezing me tightly. "I'm so sorry you had to go through that," she says in a consoling voice.

I hug her back. "I'm glad I came here."

She pulls back and gives me a small smile. "Me too. I love you."

"I love you, too."

A whine wails from beside us, so I bend down and pat Conan's head. "I love you, too."

Forty minutes later, we reach the cabin. It's small and solely made of wood. It has only a couple of windows, and it's surrounded by trees, so it blends well into the environment. We are both panting.

Elena has her arms above her head. "I'm so unfit," she says through loud breaths.

My hand goes to the sharp ache on my side. "I have a stitch."

Elena laughs. "This was your idea."

"A stupid one at that." I wipe my sweaty forehead with my arm. "I don't know if I can walk back."

She pulls the walkie-talkie out from her waistband and holds down a button. "Twitch."

"Yo," he answers.

"Can you pick us up? We don't want to walk back."

He laughs. "It's downhill."
"Please," I say loudly, hoping that he would hear.
"Give me fifteen minutes."

SEVEN

CHALLENGING TIMES

Ava

"That dog stinks!" Twitch says as we get out of the truck.

I sigh. "Yes, he does. The tap is at the back of the house, isn't it?"

"It sure is," he replies with a screwed-up face, watching my dog jump out of the truck.

"I purchased some doggy shampoo, so I might give him a wash."

"Do you want some help?" Elena asks.

My eyes scan over Conan's body. "Yes, please. I hope he'll let us wash him."

Elena's eyes widen. "He better not bite me!"

My heart is beating faster, hoping Conan won't be a problem. We walk out the back and toward the tap.

"Can you connect the hose, and I'll get the shampoo?"

Elena gives Conan a wry glance. "Okay."

I dash through the house and into the kitchen. My shoulders drop at the mess already. My fingers itch to clean it up. *If*

Beau saw our kitchen in this state . . . I cringe, then shake my head. Beau isn't here. I open the cupboards underneath the sink and grab the shampoo and comb. After walking over to the fridge, I pull the door open and get out some ham. I walk back to hear Elena laughing. She is trying to wet Conan, but he keeps chasing the stream of water from the hose, trying to bite it.

Elena looks at me. "Your dog thinks it's a game."

I smile at Conan as he bolts one way, chasing the water, and when Elena dashes the hose the other way, he follows it, barking.

"Conan, I have some food for you."

He pauses and looks at me, back to the water, then back to the ham in my hand before running to me.

Elena giggles. "The food is obviously more important."

When Conan gets to me, he jumps. "No. Sit."

"He probably doesn't know what sit means."

"Sit." I press down on his back near his tail, and he sits. His eyes never move from the food.

"Good boy." I pass him his well-deserved piece of ham, and he gently takes it from my hand and practically swallows it.

"Did he even chew that?" Elena asks.

I laugh. "No, he's a pig!" I pull out another piece of ham. "Try with the water now."

I hand the ham to him as Elena directs the water over his back. It trails down his body and drips from his belly.

"Pass me the hose and I'll do his chest."

She does, and he sits there with his doggy smile while we take turns making sure we get his coat wet. He stands, and before we can step back, he shakes himself. I close my eyes as he flicks the water all over us. We both burst out laughing.

"It's shampoo time." Conan backs away, so I quickly pull

out another piece of ham. He steps toward me. "At least he's food motivated."

Elena cocks a brow. "Aren't most men?"

I smile back at her. "True!" I give the ham to Conan, then lean down, grab the shampoo, drizzle the bright yellow liquid all over his back, and put the container on the ground. We both lean down and rub it into his coarse coat.

"Look at the color of the suds," Elena points out. It's a light brown, showing just how dirty he is.

I frown. "He's probably never been washed. Make sure you get his legs."

"I am. Check out his tail." It's wagging rapidly. "He is loving this. He's nothing but a big softie."

I put more of the thick liquid into my hand, lather it into his tail. "He sure is."

We use the hose again to wash away the suds. I hear chatter, and when I glance over my shoulder, Vera and Grace are walking by us. "Stop the water," I whisper to Elena. Her brows knit together but then her smile goes wide. And we both leap back in time for Conan to shake the water from him. Some of the water flicks onto me but nothing compared to before.

"That's disgusting," Grace hisses. "Now I'm going to smell like a dog."

The comeback is on the tip of my tongue. My eyes meet Elena's, and from the laughter dancing in her eyes, I think she's thinking the same as me. But I swallow the words.

"Stupid mutt," Vera says. She steps toward me but stops when Conan growls. "If it bites me, I'll shoot it myself."

My heart drops to my feet. My first thought is, *It's just a threat,* but her icy glare tells me otherwise. That burning anger returns, and it courses through my veins. I stand taller, pulling my shoulders back, and now it's me who's baring my teeth. "Don't you dare threaten to hurt my dog . . . or my sister."

A savage undertone lines my voice because I mean every word.

Their eyes widen. Grace steps back, but Vera studies me. "Whatever." She rolls her eyes and walks away. Grace follows.

"Well . . ." Elena says awkwardly, "you either warned her away or you just poked the bear."

"I'd say I just poked the bear."

She sighs. "I think so, too. Well, I'm going inside to have a shower."

I peer at my damp clothes. "Me too."

After my shower, I make us sandwiches and watch Elena. Her eyes keep going back to her phone.

"Is everything okay?" I ask before her phone rings.

"Hello." Her shoulders drop. "I wanted to check you were okay. It took a while for you to call me back." Elena's face falls, then she gnaws on her lip before saying, "I was worried, that's all. When will you be back?" She nods. "See you then. Love you, bye."

"They will be back either late tonight or tomorrow."

Elena goes to bed early. I hate seeing the worry in her eyes. The sweet butts are getting drunk, so I go to bed too, but I can't sleep. I pull my phone from under the pillow. I squint at the bright light and 2:05 a.m. and let out a small groan.

The best night's sleep I had was in Reaper's bed. *He's not here . . . Maybe if I get up early, I can sneak back to my bed.* I scold myself. Knowing my luck, he will walk in and catch me. I can't be sneaking into the president's bedroom, no matter how tempting it is.

"Ava," my name is called out from outside my room.

It's morning, and I haven't slept.

"Yes," I reply to what sounds like Twitch's voice.

"Can you come out here?"

Flutters of anxiousness flood my stomach. I yank the duvet off and unlock the door to see Twitch standing there. His usual casual demeanor is replaced with worry.

"Can you come into the office?"

"Okay," I reply and follow him. "Is everything okay?"

"I'm not sure," he replies, then walks into a room with computers. "Is that your husband?"

Dread feels like a heavy weight on my shoulders. I scan the computer screen Twitch is staring at, and the sight of Beau has me in a chokehold. I can't breathe.

He's found me.

My eyes can't leave the screen. It's the person in my nightmares. I can't speak, so I nod. Beau stands by his car, which is parked off to the side from the gated entrance.

"I want to talk to Ava, my wife," Beau says through the speaker by the gate.

His voice immobilizes me. He sounds concerned, but there's an undertone of anger in it. I know how fake he is in front of people.

Twitch looks at me. "Did you want me to tell him you're not here?"

I blink a few times. "Yes." My heart beats out of control.

Twitch sits in the chair in front of the computer and microphone. "I don't know who you're talking about." Amusement weaves into his voice.

Beau doesn't flinch but keeps his anger under control. "I was told she's here."

I'm quick to respond to Twitch. "No one knows I'm here." Elena would never have told him. Axle wants to punch him, and the other men didn't want to get involved.

Bomber. He didn't want me to bring my drama here. Maybe he thought Beau could take me away so they don't have to deal with it. I swallow down the vomit threatening to come up.

"Sorry, mate. They made you drive out here for no reason. She isn't here."

"I want to speak to Elena, then."

"Yeah, that's not happening. She's still sleeping."

My mind races with uncertainty. Maybe I should leave this place? What if Bomber contacts Beau again? It's the club-house of the MC men. Elena isn't one of them. I doubt her feelings hold much weight.

"Axle, Elena's husband, and the rest of the MC will be home at any moment, so I think it would be better if you left." A bite of warning punctuates Twitch's voice.

Beau doesn't reply. He walks to his car and starts it. I watch as he leaves. I can only imagine how hard it was for him to rein in his anger. I know that won't be the last I'll see of him.

Twitch swings his swivel chair around to look at me. "Who knows you're here?"

"Bomber must have told him."

Twitch laughs, making my brows furrow. "Bomber is loyal to Reaper and to the club. There's no way. Have you spoken to any family or friends?"

I shake my head. "Elena spoke to our parents, but she said she never told them or anyone else, so I don't know who it was." A heavy breath falls from my mouth. "Can you let me know if Beau comes back?"

Twitch nods. "But I don't think you will have anything to worry about. That guy won't have the balls to return."

I hope he's right. After walking out of the room, I wondered what my next move should be. I need a distraction, so I move to the kitchen and pull out the ingredients from the pantry and the fridge to make two large batches of baked omelets for the men.

My hand shakes as I grab a large dish. "Hey," someone says from behind me and I jerk, dropping it. The dish lands on the floorboards, followed by a ringing clang.

Elena curses under her breath while I apologize. "I'm so sorry."

She moves toward me, but I unconsciously step back. My arms wrap around myself. I'm on edge, and Elena frowns and slowly picks up the dish. "You have nothing to apologize for. It was an accident."

"Beau found me." The three words I was hoping I would never have to say make my eyes water.

She gasps and steps toward me, like she wants to comfort me, but stops. "Are you okay? Did you have to talk to him?"

"The gates are locked. He spoke to Twitch via the intercom, but Twitch told him I wasn't here and told him to leave."

"Okay, but how would he know?" she asks and puts her hand over her heart. "I promise you. I never said a word to anyone."

"I believe you. It must've been someone who lives here. No one else knows."

A phone rings. Elena pulls her phone out of her pocket and her shoulders slump. "It's Mom. No doubt Beau called her. I'll tell her it's a lie."

My head thumps from stress and the lack of sleep, but I go back to mixing the ingredients of the omelets, then put one in the oven.

Elena walks over and sits on a stool, her elbows leaning on the counter. "Mom doesn't believe me. She thinks you're here."

I pause before pushing the dish all the way in. I grab the

other dish and put it on the lower shelf. I shut the oven door, then turn to look at her.

Elena's hands come up. "I can't believe she believes him over me . . . Even though I am lying . . . still."

"I'm not surprised." I fold the tea towels and put them to the side. "He is persuasive."

"Maybe someone saw you shopping that day with Viper."

"I don't know anyone in this area but you and Axle, but I guess someone could have."

She shakes her head. "Axle should be home soon, so I'll talk to him about what we should do next. I don't want Mom and Dad turning up."

"I need some air. Can you check the omelets and take them out when they are golden brown on top?"

"I can do that."

"Golden brown, not black," I clarify.

She huffs. "Yes, I hear you. Don't worry, we will get all of this Beau stuff sorted."

I'm not as confident as she is. I walk toward the back of the house, open the back door, and step outside. My eyes close at the warmth from the sun, and I try to take deep breaths to calm down.

A whine draws my attention, and when I look down, Conan's glancing at me, nudging my leg. I pat his head and lean down until I'm sitting on the ground. I don't care that the small rocks dig into my skin or that the ground is hard. The weight of helplessness takes over. My hands cover my face as the tears fall.

Conan nudges me again with his gigantic head, then wetness travels up my cheek. I pull my hands away from my eyes to see Conan lean in and lick my face again. My chest warms as I cuddle him.

Rumbling motorcycles approach. Conan pulls away and barks, rushing toward the front of the house. I wipe my eyes with my hands and stand. Sniffling, I try to pull myself together. The last thing I want is for someone to see me crying.

I wander to the table and sit on the wooden bench. I wipe my eyes and cheeks again. The sound of the motorcycles gets louder. I listen closely as one motorcycle after another turns off. My throat tightens. Twitch will tell them everything. My mouth goes dry and my anxiety spikes. I should pack before I get made to leave. Save myself the embarrassment.

Making my way inside, I rush through the house and up the stairs before anyone can see me. Once in my room, I pick up my bag and open it wide. I grasp my clothes folded neatly on the bed, then place them in the bag. The men's voices get louder, and my heart beats faster.

I tense. Heavy footsteps stop in front of my room. The door is open, so I know he can see me, but I'm frozen. He gets closer until his presence looms behind me. My eyes squeeze shut, and I flinch when his arms wrap around me. His hands rest on mine, and he pulls my hands away from the bag ever so gently and pulls me into him.

With his warmth behind me, his calming presence and the caring nature of his hug break something inside of me. I sag into him and the tears come fast. He pulls me into him tighter as I sob. My body trembles, and I can no longer hold myself up. His arm comes underneath my thighs, and he picks me up with ease. He lays me on the bed and pulls the duvet over me.

He leans down, brushing the hair out of my eyes. The gesture makes me cry again, and his frown deepens. When he sits on the bed, it dips beside me. "We will keep you safe. There's no reason for you to run."

I take in the gorgeous man next to me. "Can you stay with me? I don't want to be alone."

He takes his boots off, shuts the door, and walks back. He

pulls his phone out of his pocket and it lights up. He types on it and then places it on the nightstand, pulls his gun out and sets it next to his phone. His belt and holster are next, then he sits on the duvet before lying down next to me and pulling me into his chest.

"I called my contact who is a police officer in the local district." His voice rumbles. "I told him to inform the department in charge of missing persons you will come in today to tell them you are okay and to explain why you left."

I shake my head at him. "I can't do that."

He shuffles back and lifts my chin to meet his eyes. "Tell me why."

I glance away, breaking eye contact.

He waits a moment for me to answer, then sighs. "Can you go there to show them you are okay?"

He didn't get angry or push for me to tell him, which I appreciate, but it's confusing, and my silence was almost loud.

"Being away from him seems too good to be true." My heart sinks. "I'm a coward, but . . ." My lip trembles. "I can't shake the feeling that I'm going to be forced to go back to him, and if I go back, telling the cops about what he has done will make it worse." Memories of Beau saying sorry when he saw the bruises from when he had hit me flood back, but it wasn't long after he threatened me not to tell anyone.

Reaper shuffles closer again and pulls me back into his chest. "You are courageous. He is the coward." His voice hardens at the end.

Instead of telling me to get out when I brought issues to their clubhouse, he is here, holding me. I burrow further into his chest like he's my safety blanket.

Even at the beginning of my relationship with Beau, he never showed affection or held me when I was upset. I wasted so much time on him.

When I was with him, all I wanted to do was scream. Scream for someone to help me. Scream at Beau for making me feel worthless. But I was worried about the consequences. I need to do something now. "Okay. I'll go to the police station."

He kisses the top of my head. It makes the weight of hopelessness lift slightly.

Two light knocks sound from the door, followed by Elena's and Axle's voices.

"I told you she is fine. Reaper is with her."

"She's *my* sister. I need to hear it from her."

"You stubborn woman!"

Reaper chuckles and sits up. "I'll let her talk to you. If you need me, I'll be downstairs and ready for whenever you want to go."

I shake my head and sit up, then reach over and take his hand in mine. "Please stay." His eyebrows pinch, making his forehead wrinkle. He wraps his arm around my waist, pulling me into him. "If you need me to stay, I won't leave until you ask me to."

"Come in, Elena."

She bursts through the door, her eyes bulging.

"I'm sorry, Reaper," Axle says while staring with narrowed eyes at his wife. "I tried, but when it comes to her sister, there's no talking to her."

I give Elena a small smile to reassure her that everything's okay.

"It's not a problem," Reaper replies to Axle.

Elena's eyes move to my and Reaper's hands, but then they wander to my bag and the few scattered clothes around it on my bed. She frowns. "You were going to leave?" She sounds hurt.

Axle frowns at me too. So many emotions course through

me at once, but Reaper squeezes my hand as if he can sense my feelings.

"I didn't want to cause any trouble here," I reply honestly.

"I told you we will sort it out."

"Someone from the MC contacted Beau, so I thought I wasn't welcome anymore."

"I'll find out who it was," Reaper assures me.

"We had a meeting," Axles says. "All the men agreed to you staying here. We were all aware of the implications."

It makes no sense, then. Why would someone call the police on me?

"Did you want me to go to the police station with you?" Elena asks.

I glance at Reaper. "It's okay. Reaper said he will take me."

EIGHT

STAY WITH ME

Reaper

AFTER ALL THE SHIT WE WENT THROUGH OVERSEAS IN THE military, me, Bomber, and Viper came back home and forged friendships with men who also worked in the military. Creating the MC was like finding a home. Ava makes me feel the same.

As soon as I heard her husband was here, I ran to her as fast as my feet could take me because she differed from any other woman I had met before. She's the only woman I've wanted a future with.

For the first time in my life, I ignored my instincts, the pull I had to Ava at the wedding and the connection we shared. I could sense her discomfort at how scared she was of her husband, but I still let her go. What type of man allows that to happen? I could have saved her from the domestic violence.

Whatever it takes, I'll protect her from him . . . but it's not just him I need to protect her from—it's from myself and the

MC as well. A group of men swearing and partying. It's not her scene.

We manage an illegal fighting ring and grow and distribute marijuana for a living. We are the opposite of what she needs, but I'm selfish and I can't let her go. A part of me hopes she can see past all that.

Axle said she was here, but I had to see her for myself. When I saw Ava packing her bag, the sudden assault of emotions crippled me. After everything she has been through, I didn't want to scare her. I could barely stop my hands from shaking when I gently pulled her away from her bag. Having her in my arms eased some of my tension.

"I'm nearly ready," Ava says with confidence.

My warrior.

"Make sure you have your ID."

She leans over, drags her bag across the bed, then rustles through it until she pulls out her driver's license.

"I'm going to the bathroom to wash my face, and then I'll be ready." She moves to Elena and wraps her arms around her.

When Elena opens her eyes, they glisten. She pulls back. "Please don't leave again."

"I won't," Ava replies softly. She gives Axle a small smile and leaves the room.

Elena's hands rise, covering her face, and she cries.

"Babe," Axle says, bringing his arms around her. "She's okay."

Her hands fall and so do the tears coursing down her face. "I should have checked on her. What if Reaper didn't get back when he did?"

The thought has me closing my eyes. When I open them, Elena is staring at me.

"Thank you so much."

"I won't let anything happen to her." My tone comes out harder than I intended.

She searches my eyes for a moment, then nods as if she realizes Ava means more than being Axle's wife's sister. Ever since I saw Ava, I had this pull and a loss of control that is a concern. Bad things can happen when a leader doesn't have his head on straight.

"I want her husband dead," I blurt. The dark inner part of me rejoices. I want to remove him from this earth so that Ava doesn't have to worry about him again.

Axle mashes his lips together like he's trying not to laugh. Elena's mouth goes into a straight line while horror flashes in her eyes.

"Will she hate me if I kill him?"

Elena goes quiet, lost in thought, so I wait for her answer. "She's gone through enough already. I don't want her to blame herself or feel any worse than she already does."

Disappointment slices through me. "I won't, but if he tries to hurt her in any way . . ." I shake my head. "I won't have the willpower to stop myself."

I glance at my gun. My hands itch to touch it at the thought. Having been a sniper at war, I'm used to eliminating the target, protecting my brothers. Stopping that urge will be difficult, but I'll try . . . for her.

Ava walks toward the bed and grabs a smaller bag, then places her wallet and driver's license inside of it. "Okay, let's go."

"Are you sure you don't want me to come?" Elena asks uncertainly.

"It's okay," Ava says.

I stand and put my belt on, pick up and place my gun in the holster, and grab my phone. I put my hand out, gesturing for Ava to walk out first, and then I follow her through the hallway.

"Hold on," I say as I open my door and step inside my room. I walk out to Ava. "Here." I hand her the phone. "This is yours. My phone number is already in your contacts." She stares at it. "It's a burner phone, so it can't be linked back to you."

She slowly takes it out of my hand and brings it to her face as she goes through it.

I pull out my phone and tap on my contact at the police.

"Hello," Parker answers.

"It's Reaper. We are on our way."

"I will let the investigator know. He will interview her."

I hang up, and she's staring at me.

"Thank you for the phone." Her voice is unsteady, still full of emotion.

She's an excellent cook, kind and caring and sexy as fuck. What the hell is wrong with her husband? We move down the stairs and through the house, but she halts where the keys are. "Did you want to go in the truck or on my motorcycle?"

A touch of a smile crosses her face. "I've always wanted to ride on a motorcycle."

I was hoping she would say that. After I grab my keys, we walk out the front door and head for the shed. Rage moves toward us, holding a case of beer. "Can you tell the women to get dinner ready because Ava won't be making it tonight?"

His chin lifts. "My pleasure," he says in a smug tone.

His hard work as a prospect doesn't go unnoticed. He will make a good MC club member.

In the shed, I grab Elena's helmet from the table and her leather jacket, then walk over to my motorcycle. I glance back to see Ava walking leisurely over to me, her eyes darting between me and the motorcycle.

"We can take the truck?"

She shakes her head. "No. I want to go on the motorcycle."

I open the jacket for her. "Whose is this?" she asks.

I cock a brow. "Does it matter?"

Her lips pinch. "Yes, it does."

"It's your sister's."

She nods, as if confirming that she will wear it. She slips her arms in it, and I pass her the helmet.

"It's your sister's too," I say before she questions it.

She slips it on over her head and tightens the straps. I climb on my motorcycle and stare at her. She somehow looks better than I imagined she would look like dressed in leather.

"Hop on."

She hesitates before placing her hand on my shoulder and climbing on. I lean down and point to the foot peg.

"Put your feet on the pegs and wrap your arms around my midsection." Her arms come around me loosely. "Tighter."

"What?" she asks.

I'm not sure if she doesn't understand or if she's frightened. I pull both her arms around me tighter and gently tug her calves toward me so she's flush against my back, and she lets out a small laugh. "I can't have you falling off."

Her grip around me tightens further, making me grin. I make no apologies for how turned on I am right now.

The motorcycle roars to life when I put the key in the ignition. I pull forward slowly, trying not to scare her. We go onto the dirt road, slightly bumpy from the rocks, but when we reach the asphalt, I speed up. She laughs. I fucking love it.

"Faster," she says from behind me, so I speed up. She squeals louder.

When I reach the main street of the town, I slow down and my mood plummets. When I reach the police station, I park in an empty spot out the front, then climb off and hold my hand out to her. She stares at it for a couple of seconds, then places her hand in mine. I help guide her off the motorcycle. She pulls the helmet off, and it's made her auburn hair fuzzy.

"You suit the helmet and leather jacket."

Considering what she's about to do, I see she still has a small smile on her face.

"Thank you," she replies.

It's a win in my books.

I put the helmets in the saddlebags. "Did you know you are the only woman who has been on my motorcycle?"

Her smile spreads.

It's true, and it's my way of telling her she's different from any other woman.

I glance at the police station, then back at her. All I want to do is haul her ass back on my motorcycle and get back to the clubhouse. She's been through enough already. But I had to make sure the police won't turn up at the clubhouse because they think we kidnapped her or something over-dramatic.

I stare into the distance. Is this guilt I'm feeling? I shake my head. She's not even mine, and I'm going soft already.

With my hand, I gesture toward the police station. "I've got you. You only have to answer a few questions."

I see her swallow, and that damned guilty feeling gets worse. We walk to the entrance and I open the door for her. She stands off to the side as I approach the front desk.

"I'm Reaper, and I'm after Parker."

No need for pleasantries. I don't like them, and they don't like me. The MC has an arrangement with Parker—money for information.

The woman at the desk gawks at my cut as she picks up the phone. "Parker, you have a visitor." She puts the phone down. "He will be with you in a moment."

I glance at Ava, and she hasn't moved. She's nibbling on her lip.

"Hey, Reaper," Parker says through a cheery smile as he walks to me.

I give him a sharp nod and turn to Ava. "Are you ready?"

"I am," she replies and steps toward us.

"Hi, Ava. I'm Parker. If you follow me, I'll lead you to the investigator who will do your interview."

I step forward, but Parker shakes his head. "You can't go in with her."

I scoff. "I am if she wants me to."

Parker chuckles nervously. "It's a conflict of interest. She needs to be alone, or they may think you are interfering or that your presence will influence her answers, especially since her husband has made a complaint that she is being held against her will at *your* clubhouse."

Ava gasps.

"He has no proof she's even there."

Parker breaks eye contact. "Yes, he does. He sent in photos of her there, and I can tell you now, it certainly looks like your clubhouse from when I was there last."

The thought of my men betraying my orders twists my gut.

"Ava, if you follow me." Parker looks at me and lowers his voice. "I'll meet you outside to have a chat."

I gaze at Ava. "Is that okay with you?"

Parker isn't calling the shots. She is. They've seen she's alive. Every cell in my body is screaming to return home and demand answers.

She shrugs. "I guess. I want this over and done with."

"If you don't want to answer any more questions, make sure you tell them that. If you need me, phone me. I'll be outside by my motorcycle, waiting."

"Okay," she answers and follows Parker.

As I'm walking outside, every muscle is tense. I pace by my motorcycle. How quickly a day can go to shit! My mind is scattered. I want to be in that interview room with her, and I also want to know what the hell is going on within my MC. The door opens, and Parker strides toward me.

"Do you know who has been giving her husband this information?" I snap.

I trust my men with my life, so I'm struggling to even consider that one of them has done this.

His eyes bug out, then he turns, looking from left to right, as if checking no one heard. "Keep your voice down," he mutters.

I crack my neck from side to side. "Tell me who it was."

My ice-cold voice lets out a warning. If he doesn't tell me, there's going to be consequences. One of my brothers wouldn't dare go against me . . . or the club . . . after everything we have been through . . . it makes no sense.

"Her husband forwarded the email to us. It came from your generic War Brothers MC email address."

I yank my phone from my pocket and call Twitch.

"Hey," he answers.

"Someone has accessed the computer room and emailed Ava's husband. I need to know who it was."

I glance back at Parker. "When was the email sent?"

"Yesterday."

It happened when we were away. That lowers the potential candidates.

"They accessed it yesterday." I need to find out who the traitor is because I find it difficult to believe it was Twitch or Rage. Video surveillance covers the outside of the room near the doorway.

"Ah, yeah sure. I'll get onto it now," he responds.

"I want it by the time I get home."

I clench my phone as I give my attention back to Parker. "How would anyone track her husband's email address?"

"Him and her parents have put up posters and have had her disappearance splashed all over the media in her town."

This time, I pull up Bomber's name on my phone and bring it to my ear. As soon as he answers it, I say, "I need you in the computer room with Twitch."

"I'm going there now."

"Someone accessed the computer yesterday and contacted Ava's husband, putting her at risk, so check the emails first to tell you the exact time the email was sent and cross reference it with the video surveillance to see who was on the computer at that time. I need you to go through it *with Twitch*."

"On it."

Ava walks out toward us from the entrance. I search her face, but her expression is passive so I can't tell how it went. I lean down, pull out her helmet, and hold it out in front of me with an outstretched hand. When she reaches us, she takes it from me.

"I have to go back to work," Parker says. "If I hear anything else, I will call you."

I gaze at Ava, who slips on her helmet. "We have to go home. I'll take you for a longer ride around town another time." My jaw clenches.

That's if she stays.

NINE
TRIGGERED

Ava

After Reaper helps me off the motorcycle, I notice the stress in his shoulders and the darkness in his eyes. Tension radiates off him. I've spent years analyzing Beau's behavior to tailor my own, so I have become an expert in noticing the minor details. I keep my distance but follow him.

The men cleaning their motorcycles raise their heads and smile. When they see Reaper's face, their smiles fade—they sense it too. Upon opening the front door and walking inside, Reaper marches in the direction of the computer room, making me frown.

I go through the house in search of Elena but find Cash behind the bar serving beers to Axle, Viper, and Demon.

I walk over to the side of Axle. "Hey, do you know where Elena is?"

Axle turns his head toward me and smiles. "Hey. I'm not too sure. She was here a moment ago." He scans the room. "How did it go at the station?"

The thought of the conversation I had with the officer makes me cringe. "I told him what I've been through and he suggested filing for a protective order."

Viper grunts. "Sorry, darl, but a piece of paper won't stop him."

I open my bag and grab my phone, which is cool to touch, and place it in front of Axle on the bar. "Can you put your number in it?"

He peers down. "Sure." Smirking, he picks my phone up and types. He stretches his hand out to pass it, but before I take it, Viper's hand comes out and snatches it. When he finishes, he passes it back with a mischievous look in his eyes.

I glance at my phone to see Axle, Reaper, and "Sexiest Man Alive" in my contacts. I roll my eyes, and Viper laughs.

Giggles tinkle from behind me, so I turn to see Vera and Grace walking through the house. I stiffen. A few moments later, Elena comes from the same direction. Her face is pale.

I rush to her. "What's wrong?"

Even though I'm looking at Elena, I can sense Vera and Grace approaching us.

"Did you have a pleasant trip to the police station?" Vera asks.

The smugness in her voice makes me grind my teeth. I turn, making sure that I'm in front of Elena so they can't see her anymore. "Why do you care? And, anyway, what did you say to Elena?"

That burn of anger keeps rising.

Vera looks at Grace, and they giggle again. My glare sharpens. My heartbeat is in my ears, my breathing deep and constant.

Vera leans in closer to me. "So I gather your husband got my email."

Anger tears through me. My blood's on fire and my hands are shaking.

Axle is suddenly by my side, but Viper cuts in first. "I wouldn't upset Ava. It's only going to piss Reaper off."

Vera's head swings to him, then she looks back at me, glowering with so much hatred. "You fucking bitch," she yells and lunges at me, but Axle steps between us. She looks over his shoulder. "He's mine!"

A loud laugh roars from Demon. "And you guys call me insane?" he asks, looking around at everyone. "She's a fucking headcase!"

Viper laughs, slapping his back. "No one can match your crazy."

Axle rises to his full height and gets in Vera's face. "Back down," he warns.

She steps back. Grace whispers in her ear.

When Axle looks back at us, I scowl at him. I have no patience left. "How did you not know Vera and Grace have been tormenting Elena?"

My voice is a mix of frustration and sadness. I observe Elena, frowning, hating that they have upset her. We are more alike than I realized—too nice, not wanting to cause trouble. *It needs to stop!*

"What are you talking about?" he asks.

When I glance back at him, worry is etched on his face.

"Those two," I say, pointing to Vera and Grace. Fear flashes across Grace's face. Elena's eyes dart between Axle and me. "She shouldn't have to deal with them being nasty to her in a place she calls home."

Axle's face drops. The room is silent, the tension heavy.

"Vera and Grace, pack your bags and get out of my clubhouse."

I jolt from the roar of Reaper's voice. When I peer over, it's Reaper, with Bomber standing on his right and Twitch on his left.

"I will have no one who is disrespectful or disloyal living here and especially"—Reaper's eyes cut to Vera—"someone who betrays the club."

Vera's eyes bug out, and Grace cries. I have no sympathy for them because I know I won't be missing their callous behavior.

"Ava is here for a whole of two minutes. She's not a sweet butt or an ol' lady," Vera says.

"*You* betrayed *my* orders. End of discussion," Reaper snaps at Vera. "Bomber and Demon, help them pack their bags and make them wait out the front for their ride." His dark glare remains on the women. "I never want to see your faces *ever* again."

Bomber and Demon move to them.

Demon flashes a smile at me. "I thought you were going to punch her."

His voice is full of amusement, but it has the opposite effect on me. It makes me nauseous. I was angry, but from what I've been through, I could never . . . even if I hate her. An urge to run creeps inside of me. The arguing, the yelling, and the crying are all too much, but I try to breathe through it.

Bomber and Demon escort the women up the stairs.

Axle takes Elena's hand in his. He looks at her with adoration. "I'm sorry, babe. Can we go upstairs and talk?" She nods, and they are next to go.

I can't take it anymore, and I bolt toward the back of the house.

As I leave, I hear Reaper yell, "Church in thirty minutes!"

I burst out of the back door. It bangs on the wall as I scan the area for Conan. The banging sounds must have woken him, as he's on his feet within seconds, his ears upright. His body is still until he sees me, then his tail wags.

I plop myself on the ground next to him and hug him. Tears fall from my eyes. His head nudges into me. My breathing eventually slows, and some of the tension releases.

The backdoor opens, making me stiffen, and then Reaper's towering over me. He bends over with outstretched hands, and with no hesitation, I place my hands in his. He helps me onto my feet.

He gently cradles my face in one of his hands and softly wipes one tear from my cheek. His tenderness calms me, but his hands soon fall by his sides as he steps back, giving me room. "I looked over the video surveillance with Twitch and Bomber. That's when I found out it was Vera who emailed."

"She told me she did it and seemed quite pleased with herself."

"You're not going to take off again, are you?" His voice is teasing, but his eyes don't lie.

I never thought I would feel anything for anyone after what I experienced with Beau. There is no way I can trust again, especially a man in a one-percent MC, but being with him feels right. I shouldn't judge what he does, because he's treated me better than any man.

"I'm not going anywhere," I reassure him.

The warmth in his eyes and his slow, sexy smile melt away my worrying thoughts. Being with him makes the happiness seep back in. I step toward him and wrap my arms around his solid body. His arms slide around my back and squeeze. Something about him eases the tightness in my chest. His body shifts, and he chuckles. I peer up at him and follow his line of sight to Conan, who is nudging Reaper's leg for pats.

"It looks like you have a new friend."

One of his hands falls from my back, and he leans down and rubs Conan behind the ear. "Luckily, because it seems you two come as a packaged deal."

"What's your real name?" I ask curiously.

"Bain White."

I give him a small smile. He didn't even hesitate to tell me. "I like the name Bain." It's unique but masculine. It suits him.

Amusement ghosts in his eyes. "Well, that's good, because I wasn't planning on changing it."

His head jerks down. "What is that?" Conan bolts off, and Reaper steps toward him. "Conan!" his deep voice booms.

Confused, I notice the wet patch on Reaper's jeans. It takes everything in me not to laugh while Reaper curses. "Maybe your relationship with Conan is a work in progress?" I'm struggling to keep the laughter out of my voice.

He shakes his head. "Now I've got to go have a shower, get changed *again,* and get ready for church."

I glance at his wet jeans again and burst out in a fit of laughter.

His face softens. "I'm glad you find it amusing."

I clear my throat. "Sorry, but it is pretty funny . . . For dinner, I was thinking of cooking a baked meal. Do the men eat vegetables?"

"The men will eat anything," he says as his hand goes to his stomach and a smile stretches across his face. "But it will thrill them to have a home-cooked dinner."

AFTER SPENDING OVER AN HOUR IN THE PANTRY, I SMILE AT THE food as I locate the ingredients, which are neatly organized on the shelves. I gaze at the bin beside me, which is overflowing with out-of-date food, and pull the drawstring together. The bag doesn't budge when I pull it out of the bin. I grunt and pull the bag higher, trying to wiggle it out.

A deep chuckle snaps my attention to Reaper, who's watching me. "Would you like help?" he offers.

Offended, I scowl at him. At home, I never asked for help. I did everything myself.

"I can handle the trash."

He shakes his head, then looks around at the pantry. "I don't think I've ever saw it this—"

"Clean, practical." I look at the bin again and scrunch up my nose. "You're lucky you and the other men didn't get food poisoning or end up dead. Some of that food was out of date by two years!"

His swoon-worthy smile disarms me. "We're lucky you're here, then."

On the spot, I dissolve and smile stupidly back at him.

He steps toward the bin. His biceps bulge as he easily takes the full trash bag out of the bin, and I sigh as he walks away.

My phone vibrates in my pocket, and I pull it out to see a private number calling. Hardly anyone knows this number, but my curiosity gets the better of me, so I answer it.

"Hello."

"Hi, Ava. It's Kirsty. I'm an attorney who represents the War Brothers MC. I thought I'd call and introduce myself."

"I appreciate it. Thank you, but I don't have money to pay you."

"I'm on a retainer with the MC, so unless Reaper asks you for payment, there's no bill on my side. I have been told some of your story, but I would like to discuss it in more detail in case you decide to proceed with a protective order or file for divorce. I wanted to confirm that your sister will be available if needed to corroborate your story and confirm that she saw your bruises."

Remembering that night and how upset Elena was, I cringe. "Yes, that's correct."

"I could not find further police reports of abuse. Was this an isolated incident, or has it happened before, and is it the first time you have reported it?"

"It was the first time he was physical, but he has punched the wall and broken furniture around the house," I reply weakly, knowing that if I left earlier, it may not have gotten that bad.

"Was there any other abuse, like emotional, financial, sexual?"

My breath hitches, making me cough. "All of them." I'm uncomfortable talking about this with a stranger.

"Did you tell anyone during that time? Friends, family, a counselor—or go to the hospital or doctors."

"My mom, but I can't imagine she would support me." I lean against the shelving. Besides my sister, it would be my word against Beau's. "The protective order would be a waste of time, wouldn't it?"

"Domestic violence cases are complicated and complex. I would do my very best."

"Thank you." I struggle to keep my voice even.

After the call ends, I take a moment to get myself together before I walk out. When I do, Viper is sitting on a stool at the island.

"Here she is," he says with his usual flirtatious grin. "Bomber's outside watching the pig on the spit for me. Rage and I are going to the store to get alcohol. If you need anything else for dinner, can you shoot through a message with what you need?"

"Definitely potatoes, pumpkin," I mumble to myself.

He clears his throat. "So you'll send me the list?"

I blink a few times, realizing I didn't answer him. "Yes, sorry, I will. Should I cook cauliflower and broccoli, or will it end up in the bin?"

"Cook some. Me and Rage will eat it."

I pull up a new message on my phone and type in *potatoes, pumpkin, broccoli,* and *cauliflower*.

"Hey, Ava?"

"Mmm . . ." I reply as I slowly bring my eyes up to gaze at him.

"Stop saying sorry."

"Sorry." I flinch and he chuckles, shaking his head. "I can't help it." It's ingrained in me, and I know it will take a long time to get rid of those habits.

"What alcohol do you want?"

"I'm not a big drinker, but the wine at the wedding was nice. I don't know the names of them."

"It's all right. I'll check with Elena or Axle." He yells, "Twitch, do you need anything at the store?"

Heavy footsteps get closer until Twitch comes into view. He rubs his eyebrow. "No . . . I should be fine." He was replying to Viper, but his eyes were on the pantry. He takes two more steps, then freezes. He slowly pivots, his cold eyes landing on me. "What did you do?"

Guilt strikes me, and I question myself. I shouldn't have touched their food.

"It looks better if you ask me," Viper says, as Twitch moves past me and into the pantry.

Silence.

I wait nervously, racking my brain for what I've done, but I've only chucked out expired food, and everything is organized and easily accessible.

As he walks out, I watch him closely, trying to gauge his mood as he talks to Viper. "Who's going?"

"Me and Rage are getting alcohol and whatever else Ava needs."

"I'll come and shop for the food then, and you two can get the alcohol."

Viper raises his chin. "We're leaving now. Are you ready?"

"Yep," he replies and steps over to him.

The thought of upsetting Twitch makes me feel terrible. "Did I do something wrong?"

He turns, then his face falls. He steps toward me and puts his arm around my shoulder, smiling at me. "Nah, girl." He bends down and whispers, "But next time, give me a heads-up before you do a cleanup."

"I can do that," I reply, still unsure whether I did something wrong.

THE MUSIC IS LOUDER ONCE I STEP OUTSIDE. EVEN WHILE holding the tray with a tea towel, I can still feel the heat from it. After walking over to the tables, I put the large tray down. Elena, Rage, and Axle pass by me with the other trays of food as I walk back inside.

As I grab the two jugs of gravy, Elena comes up behind me. "Is there anything else you want me to take?"

"Plates, forks, and knives." When I reach the back door, I stop and let Axle and Rage walk through first. "Oh, and napkins, salt, and pepper." I take another step, then halt. "Can you get all of the sauces too?"

Rage picks up the apple sauce and takes the lid off, then brings it to his nose and takes a deep breath. "That smells good," he murmurs, putting his finger in it.

"Rage," I warn.

He stops and looks at me with innocent eyes.

"Don't even think about it."

His shoulders drop. "What do you have this with anyway?"

"It goes on the pork."

He looks back at the jar. "I might give it a go."

I smile and continue back outside with the gravy.

After dinner, Elena and I are standing by the house, chatting.

"Did you want another glass of wine?" Elena asks.

I lift the flute to my mouth and finish the remaining mouthful. "Yes, please."

She fills it three quarters of the way, then fills her own.

"Is everything okay with you and Axle now?"

"Yes, and you were right. I should have told him earlier, but I'm the only ol' lady here and I didn't want to cause any trouble."

"Well, they are gone now. I do admit I was glad to see them go."

She turns her head, looking around outside, and sighs. "And those are no doubt the new ones taking their place."

I follow her line of sight to two new women holding cards around a table with Viper, Cash, Twitch, and the other two sweet butts. The men cheer, then one woman seductively lifts her bandeau, exposing her breasts, and throws it at Twitch's face. The men cheer again.

"Are they playing strip poker?"

"Yes. The men love it, obviously."

"The other two sweet butts who live here seem okay."

"They are. They've always been nice to me. I think they are here for a good time, rather than to claim a particular man as their own. Where's Conan? I haven't seen him since dinner."

Giggling, I point to his kennel, where he's fast asleep. "Everyone was giving him food. I think he's in a food coma."

Elena rubs her belly. "I know how he feels."

"Babe!" We turn to see Axle standing by the bonfire, waving us over. "Come sit down over here."

The fire is huge, and the closer we get to Axle, the warmer it gets. When we reach him, Elena walks into his arms and they kiss. I turn away to give them privacy and see Reaper and Demon sitting on the sandstone blocks around the fire. Demon leans back, blowing rings of smoke from his cigar. Reaper gives me a smile, so I wander over and sit on the other side of him.

"Are you having a good night?"

"I am," I reply, feeling the buzz of the wine.

"Dinner was . . ." Demon forms a chef's kiss with his fingers.

I get ready to reply, but loud motorcycles thunder up the road. Conan barks twice, then gets up out of his kennel and moves toward the side of the house.

I jump to my feet. "Conan." He stops and glances back at me. "Come here." He looks forward again and barks twice, as if he's not happy with my instructions, then makes his way over and stands beside me. "Good boy!" I pat the top of his head.

"Did you want any more wine?" Elena asks.

I raise my hand to her. "No more for me," I say through a yawn. "I'm ready for bed."

Axle puts his arms around Elena and kisses the top of her head. "We're going to bed too," he says with a cheeky wink. Elena giggles.

A familiar group of men and one woman walk beside the clubhouse and toward us. "Hey!" the president of the Kings of Chaos MC yells out to the people playing poker.

Viper glances and waves back. "Hey, man. Go grab a beer, and you can play next round."

"You three should go to bed now."

I peer back at Reaper because the lightness in his voice has gone. He looks at Axle and gestures his head toward me.

Axle steps closer. "I'll walk you up to your room."

More motorcycles echo in the air.

When the group gets closer, Conan barks, and it's deeper than it was before. It wasn't an "I'm going to rip your throat out" bark, but it was a warning.

"Demon, tie the dog up to its kennel."

Reaper's gaze hardens at me, Axle, and Elena. "I need you three gone *now*," Reaper commands.

His cold voice makes my breath seize. I snap back to my previous home, with Beau screaming at me. Tears line my eyes, and my throat tightens, forcing me to run past Axle and my sister. I faintly hear "Ava . . . Fuck!" but I can't look back. All I can do is run. My heart is slamming against my chest as I move through the house. When I reach the stairs, I grab the railing and race up as the walls feel like they're caving in.

As soon as I reach my room, I take two steps in, slam the door, and lock it. I hop into bed and cuddle the pillow as I try to catch my breath, though the tears fall hard and fast.

"Ava, are you all right?" asks Elena. The doorknob jiggles. "Let me in."

"I'm good," I croak out.

She sighs. "No, you're not. Please—"

"I am. Reaper's stern voice just . . . I don't know—triggered me, I guess."

My stomach drops from the way I acted in front of everyone. Angrily, I wipe the tears from my eyes. Beau's presence still lingers. It took one trigger for me to be back in that house, back with Beau, and, suddenly, my world came crashing down.

I sniffle and wipe my eyes again. "I'm tired. Tomorrow, we can talk."

There's a brief silence.

"Love you," Elena says, sadness tainting her voice.

She wants to help, but I don't want to talk to her about it. She doesn't understand what I'm going through, and I don't want pity.

"Love you, too," I reply.

I lie there with my mind going one hundred miles an hour. My jaw clenches as I wonder how long I will suffer. Every day without him, I'm feeling better, but now it's like I've taken two steps back. I thought if I moved and started fresh that I would be free of him and I could be me again.

The legalities are not on my mind. He can keep the house and everything in it. All I want is my life back and to smile again. I don't want to cower when he's around and suffer in silence while putting on a fake smile for everyone else.

I grab my phone from beside me and glance at it. *Great.* I've been lying here for three hours. I roll onto my other side and shuffle my body around, trying to get comfortable, though it's not working. I stare at the door and sit up, swivel around, and walk over to unlock it. I want to go to his room . . . his bed . . . to be in his arms. That's my happy place. My hand pauses on the handle. Maybe I shouldn't. He's probably angry at me from earlier.

My shoulders fall as I let out a heavy sigh. I walk back over to my bed and lie back down. Reaper's been good to me. The last thing I want to do is annoy him, especially in his room, in his personal space. I cringe. He's probably embarrassed too. Ugh! Tomorrow's going to be awful.

Footsteps thump, then two loud knocks on my door.

"Elena! I said I'm fine."

"It's Reaper."

My heart picks up pace. "It's open," I reply softly.

As soon as the door opens, I speak. "I'm so sorry for embarrassing you like that," I blurt, knowing why he's there.

Light from the moon and the bonfire casts onto him

through the window. His eyes drift over my face, and without words, he sits beside me. I stiffen. He frowns.

"I shouldn't have spoken to you that way. I'll do better."

I blink a few times in disbelief. "You're not angry?"

His brows pinch as he stares at me, then they widen and he leans back. "I'm not like your husband." He sounds offended. "Do you think I would hurt you?"

"No, no . . ." I reply quickly. "I know you're not like him. I thought I embarrassed you, so I wanted to apologize."

He pauses, and his face softens. "You could never embarrass me."

The relief is profound. I didn't realize how much it means to me for him to say that. I sit up and shuffle next to him. I wrap my arms around his middle and hug him tight as his arms go around me, pulling me to him.

"Motorcycle clubs follow different rules than society." His voice rumbles, but I don't move and stay where I am, my head on his chest. "I trust my men . . . When I told them you are off limits, I knew they would follow my orders. The men who just arrived"—he pauses, his body stiffening—"are from an MC we work with. They see you without a property cut, and to them, you are available."

I raise my eyes to him. "So that's why when they arrived you asked me to leave?"

He nods sharply. "And if they touched you." He shakes his head. "I can't afford to lose control . . . Not in front of you and not in front of another MC."

He would have protected me . . . because of Elena. "Okay."

His head tilts. "Just okay?"

"Yes, I'm so tired, but I can't sleep in here . . ." I never thought being in the arms of a biker would be where I felt safe.

His face softens, and the side of his mouth twitches, like

he's smothering a smile. "Did you want to sleep in my room?"

"Maybe I'll get a better sleep." I try to keep the relief out of my voice because I need a good night's sleep, and I don't want to be alone.

He stands and flashes me a smile while holding out his hand. I get up and place my palm in his, and head for his room. When we enter, it isn't pitch black, so I can see the bed. The bedroom is cool, the light breeze of the fan blowing on my skin. I stare at the bed longingly. The weight of tiredness hits me.

As I peek to the side, Reaper's hands grasp the bottom of his shirt, and as he brings it over his head, I blush like a teenager. My heart races as I gawk at his impressive body. My eyes follow his broad shoulders to his bulging biceps. Even his forearms are impressive. And, suddenly, I'm hit with insecurity. I'll never be skinny like the sweet butts or Elena. I got the curves and big boobs from Mom's side, whereas Elena got Dad's petite frame.

I pull the cover back and climb onto the bed. As I lie down, my body sinks into the mattress and I pull the duvet over me. I roll over to give him privacy as he gets changed but listen closely to the sound of him pulling off his jeans. The belt buckle clings as it lands on the floor. A part of me wants to turn around and see him in all his glory because I'm sure it is perfect, like the rest of him.

The shower is running, so I shuffle in bed, trying to get comfortable. I'd like to say the reason I sleep better in here is because of his bed, but I know that's not true. I close my eyes and wait for him to return.

It isn't long until the bed dips beside me, though he doesn't touch me. I take a deep breath of his cologne. The scent is unique, like roasted marshmallows with a hint of citrus and vanilla. It makes a moan slip out of my mouth. I'd usually be embarrassed, but I'm not.

"Your cologne is by far the best thing I've ever smelled," I say as I shuffle closer to him.

He opens an arm out wide, and I snuggle further into him, loving every second of being in his muscular arms.

"Goodnight, beautiful."

I can hear the smile in his voice.

TEN
SHENANIGANS

Ava

When I wake, I find myself in the same position as last night, except my leg is over his. I try my best to lift my leg slowly, not wanting to wake him, but it doesn't work. His breathing speeds up and he turns his head, his eyelids heavy.

"How was your sleep?" he asks in a deep, sleepy voice.

I sigh with relief. "Much better."

"Me too," he replies.

"I'd better get up and start breakfast," I say as I sit up in bed and scoot over, putting my legs over the edge of the bed.

"Don't worry about it. We have plenty left over from last night."

I stand and turn to him. "It's my job."

"I'll pay you your leave entitlements."

I crack a grin. "Well, in that case, I'll go down and clean. I can only imagine the sight of it from last night." It makes me cringe.

"You love it!"

My chin lifts. "There's nothing wrong with having a clean kitchen."

He looks at me with warmth in his eyes. "It's been great having you here."

Happiness ricochets right through me. "Did you want me to help with anything else today?"

"Hmm . . ." His eyes flare in recognition. "I do, actually."

I stare at him, waiting for an answer. "I want you to rest and—"

"I don't think so . . . and what else?"

"Can you check out the window to see if the clothes are still on the line?"

I step over to the window. "They sure are."

"They don't even cook anymore, and they still can't get the clothes off the line." Annoyance coats his voice.

"Don't worry, I'll get them."

He smiles. "No, it's fine, I will."

I proceed to the door but pause and turn to face him. "I'll do your washing for you from now on." I walk out. Other women touching his clothes is not something I like.

After getting the leftovers ready for breakfast and finishing cleaning up the kitchen, I walk outside to greet Conan, who's sitting by his kennel. In my hand is the leftover food scraped off people's plates. When he sees me, his tail wags. He stands and stretches before walking over to me, then sniffs the air as the food catches his attention.

"Sit!" I say firmly. When he does, I place the plate in front of him. He stares at it with bulging eyes and drool coming from his mouth. "Eat!" He stands and goes for it—well, rather, shovels it in.

The back door opens, and Reaper walks out. When he sees me, he smirks and shakes his head. "You're going to make that dog obese."

Offended, I drop my jaw. "He was too skinny before!"

Reaper's eyes lock onto Conan's stomach. "I'd say he's caught up."

I stare at Conan's belly. *Oh, damn. He has a point.* Conan will have to be taken for a walk again. I frown, thinking about how much of a bad idea that was before.

"What's wrong?" Reaper asks when he sees the distress on my face from the thought of having to exercise.

"Twitch had to come get me, Elena, and Conan last time we went for a walk."

His head tilts to the side in bafflement. "Why?"

"Me and Elena couldn't walk home." I cringe at how lazy and unfit we sound.

His laugh is loud. "You two couldn't or didn't want to?"

"Oh, no we couldn't! Conan loved it, though."

"Viper and Rage go running most mornings. Why don't you ask them if they will take him?"

I shift uncomfortably.

"Conan will be fine," he answers like he can tell I'm not sure about the idea.

"I know. I feel like an overprotective mother."

He steps over to me, puts an arm around my waist, and places a tender kiss on the top of my head. The small display of affection makes my pulse spike. Being with him is easy. He's not overbearing. I'd love to spend more time with him.

"The fights in the warehouse are on tonight."

My head snaps up to him. "Who's fighting?"

"Rage."

"No!" I reply sharply.

He leans back with an odd expression on his face. "What do you mean, no?"

"I've grown fond of the men here. Them getting hurt"—I rub my eyes—"stresses me out!"

His hand moves up and down in a soothing motion. "No

one is making Rage do anything he doesn't want to do. He enjoys it."

"He's too young. I thought Demon would be into something like that."

"I won't allow him to compete."

"Why?" I thought he would be a perfect competitor from what Elena has hinted at.

"We make money from running and organizing the fights, so including a prospect allows for a level playing field with the other competitors from around the area and others who travel from around the state. Viper and Bomber have specialist hand-to-hand combat skills, and anyone who knows about our MC will have heard about Demon's reputation. No one would be stupid enough to compete against them, and if there's no competition, there's no money."

I nod slowly, now understanding the thought process behind it. "You're running it as a business."

"Yes. Now, we're going for a ride to the Kings of Chaos clubhouse this afternoon. Do you need anything while I'm out?"

A tick of nervous energy zaps me. It seems every time that MC is around, there's conflict or tension, but I try to forget about it because I've only seen them twice. "No, I'm good, but I might see if Elena is free. I wouldn't mind going to get some more clothes."

"Take Rage or Twitch with you."

My eyes dart away.

"Hey," he whispers and tucks a strand of hair behind my ear. The tender touch makes me look at him. "It's for your and Elena's safety."

"Okay." Even though it's weird having a bodyguard around with us.

"Sometimes my voice comes out harder than I intend it to,

but if I upset you, I need for you to communicate that with me. Honesty is important to me."

"It's important to me too." I could never communicate how I felt because I didn't want to make the situation any worse than what it was with Beau. "It wasn't just your tone." My hands fidget in front of me. "If it sounds like you're giving me a command, I struggle with it. I know you're not Beau and that you have my safety at the forefront of your mind, but it's hard to rewire years of feelings, so bear with me."

He kisses the top of my head again. "I should have known. I'll do better." He steps away and walks over to the clothesline.

I shake my head, feeling confused about "I'll do better." I don't know if he will understand how much relief that gives me. I watch on, grateful that I've found him. Reaper is the man all women want. Good-looking, loyal, supportive, and kind. He looks like a savage beast of a man but treats a woman like a queen and with the utmost respect. I never thought men like him existed, and it blows my mind that he's interested in me.

He takes his shirt off the line, then he turns to face me, and when his eyes pierce mine, a slow grin appears. My stomach is in knots as he prowls toward me with a shirt in hand. My breathing quickens when he reaches me, and I can't take my eyes off his lips. I stand on my toes and wrap my arms around his neck as he bends down, pressing his lips to mine. They are soft but firm, and I close my eyes and let myself enjoy him.

Reaper's arms are around my waist, pulling me tighter against his hard body. Parting my lips, I deepen the kiss, tilting my head to give him better access. His silky tongue dances with mine. I moan as heat spreads through my body, but he slows the kiss, then smiles against my lips.

I pull back, my breath ragged, but I can't resist the urge to press one last kiss on his lips before I bring my heels to the ground and reluctantly drop my arms from his neck. "Have a safe ride." I smile as my head spins.

His chest buzzes with laughter. "I could get used to that." His smile falls, and he looks at Conan, who's running away. "Conan!"

I peer down to see another wet patch on Reaper's leg.

There's deep laughter, and I peer over to see Viper with his head back in hysterics. "Hey, Pres, no disrespect, but I think Conan's trying to mark his territory."

Reaper's eyes narrow to slits. "And what's that meant to mean?"

Viper lights up, clearly enjoying this. "You're his bitch!"

I burst out laughing, while Viper dashes back inside.

Reaper chuckles lightly, but I hear "fucking prick" under his breath.

"Tsk-tsk. You need to get your men under control," I taunt.

"That's an impossible task. I'll put the money we owe you in your room. Did you want me to put it anywhere in particular?"

"At the front of my bag will be fine."

"I'll do that now." He cuts Conan with a glare and says, "And go change my jeans." He peers back. "I'll see you later, beautiful."

Licking my lips, I check him out as he saunters away, thinking all I want is to have his lips on mine again.

After I fill up Conan's water, I go inside and see Elena at the fridge, pulling out a bottle of water.

She closes the fridge door, and when she sees me, she asks, "Did Conan pee on Reaper's jeans again?"

I giggle and nod twice. "I shouldn't laugh, but I can't help it."

"That's so funny. I wonder why he does it, and only to Reaper."

"I have an idea."

Her eyes widen. "Tell me!"

"I have a feeling Conan's showing his unhappiness with Reaper and I getting close."

"If that's the case, the men are going to *love* tormenting Reaper. Conan's food motivated, so maybe Reaper can buy him a steak to win him over."

"That's not a bad idea! It might work. On that, can we go to the store today? Reaper paid me, so I wouldn't mind getting some clothes, but after that, I'm hoping to save more money."

Her smile fades. "You're saving up to leave already?" She peers down, rubbing her arm. "I was enjoying having you around."

"No. Actually, the opposite. I was going to ask Reaper if I could stay for a while so I could pay for a chef course in community college because, if I get in, I don't think I'd be able to afford the course and pay for accommodation and everything else."

She claps, her face instantly brightening with a wide smile. "Oh, that's amazing news! I remember you saying you wanted to cook professionally. You're going to kill it, and you can practice all your new skills and recipes on us."

"I was worried about leaving Beau. I never thought any of this could be a possibility, and, honestly, I'm so grateful for everything you and the MC have done for me."

Motorcycles whir, then speed up as the sound of their exhausts gets more distant.

"What's going on with you and Reaper?"

I inch back, surprised by her question. "I don't know. He's great, but . . ."

"What's wrong?"

I slump down on the stool and confess. "I'm not skinny like all the other women here, and I come with baggage. I'm not even sure if I'll ever recover from what I've been through. Why would he want that? Why would anyone want that?"

She slips her arm around my waist. "You need to stop putting yourself down. Everyone has baggage. You're an incredible person. You have a big heart, and everyone adores you."

I smile weakly. "Thanks, but you're my sister, so you're biased."

"Stop it!" she warns. "I've never seen Reaper care about a woman before. Axle said that Reaper's loyal and has always been there to support every man in the clubhouse. Axle said he will treat you the same. He hasn't rushed you into anything, has he?"

"Now that I think about it, he let me make the first move when it came to kissing and sleeping in his bed."

She nods as if happy with my answer, but her eyes go wide, and she points at me and scowls. "And don't you dare talk about your body like that again! I think it's unfair you got all the boobs and ass." She looks down at her breasts, then back at me. "I think you got both of ours." We both laugh at that. "Reaper's got the best of both worlds."

My insecurity lessens. "I didn't think of it like that."

She points to under her eye. "Look!"

I lean in further, not sure of what I'm supposed to be examining. "I don't see anything."

"My first fine line. The wrinkles have begun."

She sounds devastated, but I see no line.

I snort. "You're still in your twenties. Don't be ridiculous."

She rolls her eyes. "How can you not see the line there?"

"At least *I* don't have to worry about wrinkles."

She quirks a brow. "Hmm, and why is that?"

"Fat don't crack, baby!" I say with a wink.

She smothers a laugh before her face falls back into seriousness. "You're not fat!"

A phone rings, and I know it's Elena's because it's a Cardi B song. She brings it to her face, grimaces, but doesn't answer it. She just lets it ring. She peeks at me from under her eyelashes, then back down at her phone.

"It's our parents, isn't it?"

She smiles sadly. "Don't worry, I won't answer."

I let out a long sigh. "It's okay, I'll talk to them."

Her brows rise high. "Are you sure? You don't have to."

My hand comes out as I wait. She hesitates before putting her phone in my hand. I answer it. "Hey, it's me, Ava."

"Ohhh . . ." I have to pull the phone away from my ear at Mom's squeal. "Ava, finally. What happened? Why didn't you call us?" Her voice is filled with concern.

Guilt leaves as quickly as it came. "I told you things weren't good between me and Beau."

There's a momentary silence.

"But it's a marriage. You don't leave when it gets tough." The clip in her tone makes me choke. I have to pat my chest to get my bearings. *Did she really just say that?*

"He hit me. That isn't what a loving marriage is about."

"He told us he accidentally pushed you and you fell. He feels terrible. Look, you just need to give it some time. You two will work it out."

"He said that, did he?" I ask, spitting venom. That distinct burn fires through me. "He lost control and hurt me," I say, louder this time. "I was black and blue. How can you defend a man that abuses his wife? I'm your daughter! In what world am I the villain and he's the victim?"

She breathes heavily through the phone. "You know I love you, but you're saying he hit you, and he's saying he accidentally pushed you. Then you leave without a word. Is it possible that you misconstrued the situation, thinking the accident was deliberate?"

My heartbeat is frantic, and my breathing is out of control. I'm desperately trying to reign in my emotions. "Why aren't you listening to me? He is lying to you. I refuse to live like that anymore. He controlled every aspect of my life and made me miserable. I want the parts of me he stole. I want to be happy again."

"Beau has been over here every day, seeing if we have spoken to you. He was crying, Ava. If he doesn't reconcile with you, he's thought about killing himself. He's sorry, and he loves you."

I laugh, but it's cold and flat.

"There's nothing funny about this!" Her tone is curt.

"They were crocodile tears, and I don't believe him. It's the ultimate manipulation, threatening to kill himself, so that I'll return. He shows you what he wants you to see. You haven't met the other side of him. He didn't love me. He liked to control me. He's mentally ill, Mom. He needs help."

I'm baring my soul to her, but I wonder if it's a waste of time.

"How do you have empathy for him and not for me?" My voice is uneven as I struggle not to cry. "Would he have to beat me so bad that I'm hospitalized or dead for you to understand how dangerous he is?"

She sniffles and a muffled voice chimes in, "Ava, it's Dad. Your mom's very upset about everything."

"She's upset?" I ask in a high-pitched tone. I'm the one tormented in a domestic violence relationship for years, so how are my mom and Beau more upset than me?

"She has been beside herself since you left. We put up posters and were calling around town. We were so worried."

"I'm sorry for worrying you, but do you understand that this is the reason I never called? You two are encouraging me to go back to an abuser. You would rather me be unhappy or end up dead so no one in the church finds out your daughter left her husband."

"How could you say that?" he asks, sounding offended.

"Beau will not change! I want to feel safe, and I want to be loved. Why won't you support that?"

"You're going from a person who you said abused you to staying with a motorcycle gang? You must see how that is hard for us to comprehend. One day you're smiling with Beau, and the next we find out you're having an affair with a biker."

"Excuse me? What makes you think that?"

"A woman who was living in the MC ended up connecting with Beau, and she said you were with the president of the MC called Reaper. *Reaper . . . really, Ava?*"

I think back to Vera. She's a pain! But I'm not embarrassed at being close to Reaper, either.

"Of course he told you," I reply sarcastically. "Well, Dad, you know it's bad when I have to go to an MC clubhouse for safety and that man *Reaper*," I mock in the same tone he used, "has treated me better than Beau ever did."

He lets out a long sigh. "We miss you. When are you coming home? You can stay with us."

Holding the bridge of my nose, I take two breaths before answering. "You live in the same town as him, and you welcome him into your home. There's no way I am going anywhere near him. I'm getting a divorce."

Dad sighs again. "Your mother won't be happy about that."

"I'm the one who has gone through hell. If you want to talk to me, I guess you two will have to come to the clubhouse and then you can see *both* of your daughters."

There's a pause.

"We love the both of you . . . I'll try to get your mother there."

Good luck with that, I think.

"I love you."

My hand rubs down my face. "I love you, too, Dad. Bye."

I hang up and pass Elena's phone back to her. Her smile is wide and she claps slowly. "Well, you sure told them!"

Anger, disappointment, and annoyance clashes inside of me. "I shouldn't have to explain why I don't want to stay married to an abusive husband. Going against their beliefs is one thing, but Beau has been going over there every day, trying to make our parents believe me and him can overcome it. I'm getting treated as if I'm blowing all of this out of proportion."

Elena sits up straighter, then blinks rapidly as if she's trying to process what she's hearing. "Are you serious?"

"Beau plays the part of the victim so well I could vomit."

"He needs to get over it and move on with his life." She cringes. "God help the next woman he ends up with."

A shiver travels through my body, and I glance at the goose bumps on my arms. "No one should go through what I had to go through. I don't want it to ruin our day. Did you want to go shopping now?" I ask as Twitch passes us, going into the kitchen.

"I'm ready," Elena replies.

I walk over to see Twitch and find him in the pantry. I can hear him unwrapping something. He's hunched over, stuffing something in his mouth. I peer around him. He's holding a big box with anchovies written on the side. I step back, not wanting to interrupt his feast, but he stands straight and slowly, then turns around while chewing, and it takes everything in me not to laugh. He has chocolate on the side of his face near his lip.

He swallows his food. "Don't tell anyone where my stash is, since you chucked out my last box!"

My mouth gapes open. "I knew something was wrong with you that day. You should have told me. I chucked everything that was out of date."

"What was *in the box* was perfectly fine."

Elena walks in, and her eyes bulge. "YOU better share that, or I'll tell everyone you've been holding out on us."

His gaze sharpens, and he shakes his head at her, then glances at me. "Your sister's not being very nice, making threats like that."

"You're not very nice!" Elena says to him. "Do you know where Rage is? We want to go shopping."

"He'll be getting ready for tonight. I'll take you." He wraps up the top of his precious chocolate and puts it back in the cardboard box marked as anchovies. He pulls out the rice and puts the box at the back of the shelf. He places the rice in front of it.

I bite my bottom lip as I smother a laugh at the effort he is going through to hide chocolate from everyone.

"I'll meet you two at the truck." He shoots a wary glance at Elena.

Elena and I go to our rooms.

I pull out my bag and unzip the front section. As I pull out the notes, I gasp. This is way too much. I take one hundred dollars out of it and place the rest back, making a mental note to give it back to him. I open the top of the bag, take out my wallet, and place the money inside it. I get up and close the door behind me. I hurry along in case they are waiting for me.

When I open the back door, there's no sign of Elena, so I take a seat in the truck and close the door.

"If you were so worried about your chocolate, why don't you store it in your room or somewhere private?"

When Twitch glances over his shoulder from the front seat, he's smirking at me. "Because I have no self-control."

"So you sneak into the cupboard and hope not to get caught?"

His hand goes to his chin. "I guess I do, but did you know anchovies are one of the most hated foods in America?"

"No, I did not know that."

"See!" He gives me a playful glare. "It was a *perfect* plan!"

"You know you'll have to find another hiding space. Elena will tell Axle."

He lets out a long groan. He turns the ignition at the same time that I see Elena approaching the vehicle. When she gets closer, the truck jolts forward and stops. I'm grinning, knowing what Twitch is doing. Elena stamps over, but the truck accelerates, making me giggle.

"Twitch!" Elena yells.

The doors lock as she walks over to us again.

"Twitch! Open the door," she warns, with a hint of amusement in her voice.

I lean forward in my seat to get a better view of their bickering.

His window slides down. "Yes, Elena, how can I help you?" Smug and oh so cheeky!

"Let me in the truck."

"Hmm . . . it depends."

"On what?" she asks with suspicion in her voice.

"If you're going to tell Axle or anyone else where my chocolate is."

There's silence.

"Okay, fine . . . I won't."

"You won't what?"

"I won't tell Axle or anyone else where your stash is."

The doors unlock.

"Well, hurry up, then. I don't have all day."

THE SHOPPING WAS UNEVENTFUL. TWITCH WAS IN SURVEILLANCE mode, scanning every store we went to.

As we drive back into the driveway, my eyes skim the clubhouse. The men's motorcycles aren't there, so they still aren't home yet.

"How long do the men usually stay at the other MC for?"

"Not too long. Why?" Elena asks, then smirks. "Are you worried?"

"No . . ." I answer and see Twitch watching me in the rearview mirror. "Maybe . . ." I answer truthfully. "The way Reaper's mood changed when that MC was here was unsettling."

The truck comes to a stop out the front. We get out and move to the back to get the bags.

"I can't believe you're going to be living here . . . with me!" Elena squeals and jumps up and down.

"Let's take it one day at a time."

A part of me is scared—disturbed, even—that I would think of being with someone else so fast. But by being with Reaper, I'm feeling like the old me again. Or better yet . . . the new me.

"Well, if Reaper didn't bag you, someone else would have. We weren't letting you go anywhere."

My mouth falls open at the compliment—or the insinuation of a suggested kidnapping. "I know you're joking, but when talking to a woman, maybe . . . think about your choice of words."

He gives me a lopsided grin. "It's a good thing. You're a catch!" He playfully elbows me as he takes about eight bags in two hands.

There's the distinct sound of motorcycles, and it's like music to my ears.

"They're . . . back!" Elena says in an upbeat voice.

We get the rest of the bags out, and Twitch parks the truck while we wait for the men. They come in single file, and it's the first time I notice their custom bandanas covering the bottom half of their face. They all have similar skulls, but each has their own personalized edition.

As the men park, I squint to get a better look. Reaper has the grim reaper, Viper has a snake intertwined through the skull, Bomber has fire around the skull, and Demon has a scary skull with horns, which I assume is a demon. I have to take a few steps to my right to see Cash. His bandana has a skull surrounded by dollar signs.

Reaper walks toward us, his hair flipped in different directions from the helmet.

I giggle to myself. "Can you bend over and—"

A loud laugh interrupts me. Then I see Axle with his arm around Elena.

"It's always the quiet ones you have to be careful of." He gives Elena a pointed look, and her jaw drops, eyes bulging.

She whacks his chest and goes bright red. "I have *never* asked you to bend over!"

"It's okay, baby," he purrs. "You don't have to lie to them. No judgment here."

Elena looks like she's about to die from embarrassment. She smacks him twice more. "Stop lying!"

He laughs. I cringe. I don't want to hear about what goes on in their bedroom.

"You couldn't help yourself, could you?" I ask Axle.

Amusement swirls in his eyes. "Don't be like that . . . I'm your favorite brother-in-law."

"You're my *only* brother-in-law," I deadpan.

"You've been spending too much time with Viper. He's rubbing off on you," Reaper says.

Viper strides forward beside Axle. "I heard my name."

They keep walking, but I tug Reaper's arm to get him to stop. When he does, I stand on my toes. He tips his head forward, and I run my hand through his hair, trying to tame it. It's like silk between my fingers.

"There," I say. "Much better."

His genuine smile hits me right in the chest, but it's the flash of heat in his eyes that makes me blink a few times to check it was real. As we walk inside, he asks, "How are you coping with the swearing and all the shit-stirring between the men?"

I shrug. "I'm not a fan of the swearing, but it doesn't bother me, and I try my best to ignore anything sex related that comes out of their mouths."

"It's only friendly banter. The men can't help themselves."

Axle and Viper come straight to mind.

"I noticed."

"The fight's on later, but we'll be leaving soon to check the warehouse is ready."

I frown, thinking about Rage fighting, but I try to hide it by changing the subject. "Did you want dinner?"

"Most of us won't be here. I'll give you money to order pizza. I pay them extra to come out our way. Leave the boxes in the fridge, and some of us will eat it when we get home."

I shake my head, narrowing my eyes at him. "On that, you gave me way too much money. So I'll use it to get the pizzas."

He snorts. "Like hell you will. It's your money. You earned it."

"You overpaid me!" My mouth presses into a hard, flat line as I exhale through my nose. "I want to earn my way and be independent. It's important to me."

"I understand—"

"But?" I ask, beating him to it. He's not taking me seriously. The humor in his eyes only proves me right.

"I'm not having you pay for dinner. The MC paid you what you earned, and I put in the rest."

My eyes widen. "That makes it worse!" I screech. "I'm getting the money now and giving it back to you."

As I turn, he grasps my wrist. "I have heaps of money, and I want to help you."

With a shake of my head, I tell him, "You've done too much already, and I can't take money off a man." I peer at the ground. "Not again." I have to earn my own way and anyway, I'm not *that* person who takes and takes and takes.

His hands move to my cheeks, tilting my head up. His eyes are intense as they gaze into mine. Up close, the gold flecks sparkle in his hazel eyes. "I. Want. You!"

I gasp, surprised by his forwardness. "Why?" He could have anyone.

"I was in the military. I always trusted my instincts, and they never let me down, so I'm not going to stop now. From the moment I saw you, I knew you were different. Tell me, did you feel anything for me when we first met?"

I hesitate. He says nothing, just waits for me to talk. "Yes, I did."

"And now, how do you feel?"

I swallow thickly as my heart hammers. "Those feelings are stronger now."

He slowly nods. "I'm not going to rush you, but I'm hundred percent in this. I don't give a shit about money, but I care about you, so whatever's mine is yours. I've got your card linked up to my account. I've already organized and picked it up."

I open my mouth, but nothing comes out, so I shut it.

"Don't overanalyze it. The money is there for you whenever you need it. All I want is to see you happy."

His hand goes to the back pocket of his jeans, and he pulls out his wallet, opens it up, slides out the black-and-gold card, and hands it to me. I stare at it, and sure enough, my name is on it. I blink in disbelief. He leans down, placing a soft kiss on my lips as his hand touches my hip.

When he pulls away, he smirks. "I've got to get going." He peers down. "I've put the card in your pocket."

Emotion chokes up my throat. I'm worried that if I talk, I'll cry. It's not about the money; it's his trust and faith in me . . . in us. I've been trying to deny my feelings because I thought it was too soon, but he's the reason I've been able to keep my head above water since I've been here.

As he walks away, I clear my throat. "Reaper." He turns. "Can we go for that motorcycle ride you promised me?"

The corner of his mouth curves, flashing white teeth. His smile instantly calms me, making the remaining negative energy fall away.

"We can go tomorrow."

Rage walks in wearing shorts and no shirt. I keep my eyes above his shoulders. Viper's hands go to Rage's shoulders, and he shakes him. "You psyched up for your fight?"

Rage laughs and steps away from him. "Get off me."

"I want some," Viper says, rubbing his fingers together, making the money gesture and swaying his hips. "Money, money, money."

"You need help! That's what you need."

Viper kisses the air, and Rage shakes his head and laughs again.

Viper claps and yells out, "Come on, let's go win us some money, boys!"

Cheers roar, then they walk out the front door. When the last person walks through and the door slams shut, I run straight to Reaper's room. My heart pumps quickly as I hurry up the stairs. When I get into his room, I dart over to the bed, jump onto it, and land on my back. I cackle to myself. I forgot how good it feels to smile . . . to be seen . . . to feel appreciated. Their motorcycles start up, and they take off. I pull my phone from my pocket and look up the local pizza spot, place an order, then set my phone beside me. I snuggle further into his pillow and close my eyes with a smile.

My eyes flutter open at the faint sound of a door opening and closing, so I know Reaper's home. The bed dips beside me, and he shuffles over behind me until his body is flush against mine, making me smile. His arm comes around me, holding me, and he places a soft kiss on my shoulder.

"Mm . . ." I mumble, still sleepy, but then remember where he's been. "Is Rage okay?"

"He's fine, and he won. Sorry for waking you. Go back to sleep."

And I do just that.

ELEVEN
I NEED HIM

Ava

At lunch time, Reaper and I leave to go on our first date. As we walk into the restaurant, the hum of voices hushes when we step inside. I feel everyone's eyes on us. I survey the room, and I'm correct. This is a beach town, and everyone is dressed casually, like they have just walked in from the shore. I straighten my boho dress.

"I'll be back," I say to Reaper, pointing to the restroom sign. I walk in, hoping that by the time I return everyone will be back to their conversations. While I wash my hands, I glance at my face and smile stupidly at the state of my hair from the motorcycle ride. I pat down my hair.

A couple of months ago, if someone told me that my new favorite hobby would be on the back of a motorcycle, that my best friend would be a dog, that I would be close to my sister again, and that I would be dating a sexy biker, I would have laughed in their face and told them they were crazy. Yet here I am.

I hook my bag strap over my shoulder and walk out. I have to walk slowly because of the two men, who came from the men's restroom, staggering in front of me. They are very intoxicated. When they take a seat, I can see better, so I scan for Reaper. When I see him, I move toward him until a leg comes out in front of me, making me stop.

"Aren't you something?" the man slurs.

They look young—maybe midtwenties. The speaker's glassy eyes slowly travel up and down my body.

I stiffen at first, but then a burn of annoyance makes me glare at him. "Can you move your foot . . . please?" I try to be polite, but there's a distinct edge in my tone.

He chuckles and looks at his friend. "She's got manners too."

"Have we got a problem here?" Reaper growls.

The place quietens, and I feel eyes on us. Both drunk men gawk at Reaper with wide eyes, then sink into their seats. The man with his leg out moves it, allowing me access.

"No, no problem," they repeat, shaking their heads.

Reaper's gaze warms when he glances at me. His eyes study my face as if to see whether I'm in any distress.

"Were they harassing you?" He's eerily calm, but I sense it's a front.

The men peer up at me with big doe eyes, like they're silently praying I say no.

"They were rude," I say to Reaper, then glance back at them. "But they were just going to apologize. Weren't you?"

"Yes, yes. Sorry, ma'am," one says, then the other.

"We are very sorry." The man looks up at Reaper. "We didn't know she was yours."

I glower at them with a twisted scowl. That saying does not sit right with me. I'm not property, but . . . I am his, and he is mine.

Reaper's eyes are on me, and he's watching me closely, so

I stand straighter. "Well, I am," I say boldly. "So watch what you say when you're speaking to a lady. You just don't know who her partner is."

"Yes, ma'am," they say in unison.

I give them a sharp nod, feeling empowered by the interaction, and when I step over to Reaper, he gazes at me with a devastating smile on his face. As we move to our table, the two men leave. When Reaper and I take a seat, his eyes roam the top half of my body. When his eyes return to mine, the heat of his gaze makes my insides coil.

"That dress . . ." he says, shaking his head with the hint of a smirk. "You look unbelievably sexy."

I glance down at the dress and smile. I wore it because I wanted to look as good as I feel. My eyes scan the restaurant. I'm glad *most* people aren't paying attention to us anymore. He passes me a menu, and I skim it. Once I've made my decision, I look around.

"It's nice here."

It has an industrial, rustic look. To the far right are exposed bricks. The chairs are simple black steel, but the tabletop is a mix of different shades of wood.

A young female server comes to our table. She smiles at me, but when her eyes land on Reaper, they widen before she pastes a fake smile on her face. "Hello, my name is Cassie. I'll be your server for today. Would you like a drink?"

"A water," I reply.

"Beer."

She gives us a sharp nod. "Have you decided on your lunch, or would you like more time?"

I peek at Reaper. "Are you ready to order?"

"Yes." He looks at the server. "I'll have the pork ribs."

"Chicken burger for me. Thanks."

She writes it down on her pad, giving us a polite smile. "Great. I'll go get your drinks for you."

He looks at me with a raised brow.

"What?"

"I thought you would have ordered something fancy."

I fight to keep a straight face. "Sometimes you can't beat the classics. So . . . tell me something about yourself." I inwardly cringe at how lame that sounds.

He leans back in his seat. "What do you want to know?"

"Why the nickname Reaper?"

He scratches the back of his neck. "You sure you want the answer to that? It might change the way you see me."

My stomach drops, but I want to know. "Please tell me."

He shifts in his chair, looking uncomfortable, making my stomach drop further. "During our tours, they called me Reaper because the grim reaper is death. They gave me targets to take out, and I was very good at my job."

"Is that all?"

His lips partially open as he tilts his head. "What did you think it meant?"

Before looking at him, I look away. "I don't know what I expected, to be honest."

"My turn," he says with a devious smirk. "What's your plans over the next two years?"

I've never been asked that question before, but then I never thought I'd do or be anything other than a housewife. "I am going to apply for a chef course at a community college."

"You know there's a college about fifteen minutes from here."

"Yes. That's the one I was looking at applying to. I was going to speak to you about staying at the MC while remaining the cook there so I can afford to pay for college."

He studies me. "The MC *is your* home."

Joy fills my heart at his words . . . home. "I admit, it feels like home."

"Your home is also in my bed . . . with me." His expression is dark but sexy.

I clench my thighs together and laugh it off. "Yes, your bed is very comfortable."

He clears his throat and raises a brow. "And what about me?"

"You're *okay*, I guess," I reply coyly.

His face falls. "Okay?" He raises his brows, sounding offended. "*Just* okay?"

"I'm only there for the comfortable bed," I joke, amused at his reaction.

He leans forward and squeezes my thigh under the table, making me jolt. With a smile, he answers, "I think you're a little liar."

I smile widely back at him as the server appears at our table, putting the drinks in front of us.

"Can I order a rare steak to go as well? The biggest that you've got," I ask.

"I'm sorry," she asks, looking confused. "Can you repeat that?"

"I want to take a steak home for the dog."

She giggles as she writes it down on her notepad. "I'm sure we can organize that for you."

Reaper shakes his head. "You want to hope Viper and Rage will take your dog for a run because if you feed him the way you're going, he may struggle to walk."

I like the way he doesn't mention the cost but mentions the health of my dog, when I'm sure he doesn't even like him. Just puts up with him because of me.

"The steak is for you to give to Conan."

He blinks in disbelief. "Why would I do that?"

"Me and Elena were talking about it. Conan is food motivated. It could be a peace offering."

He snorts. "I guess anything is worth a try to stop him pissing on my leg."

I burst out laughing, holding my stomach as I remember the wet patches on his leg and Conan sprinting away. Once I have controlled myself, I say, "Next question! Have you been married or had a longtime girlfriend?"

"No," he responds swiftly.

"Why?" When I look around, a group of ladies is watching us—well . . . watching him. "You have plenty of admirers. I'm sure it would be easy for you to get a woman."

He shrugs. "It was never a priority. I was overseas all the time, and I saw men who struggled to be apart from their wives and children. I didn't think it would be fair, and I didn't want the distraction, either."

"But you've been home for a while now. Haven't you been in any relationships?"

His deep frown twists my gut. "We were all messed up for a while when we came back, and then I put all my time and energy into the club to make it what it is today. I'm president, and the men rely on me and trust that I make the best decisions for the club, and I wanted nothing to interfere with that."

A lump in my throat makes it hard to keep my cool. "And how do you feel now?"

Reaper's hand comes out, reaching across the table and putting it on mine, and it settles some of the unease. "Seeing Axle and Elena together opened my eyes that it is possible to have a partner while still managing club responsibilities. Then I saw you at the wedding, and I had never wanted someone else so bad."

"So it was love at first sight," I tease.

"No doubt about it, beautiful."

Our lunch arrives, and during the meal we are engrossed in conversation, but every time I glance at the women's table, at least one is blatantly staring at Reaper. I get it—he's sexy and hard not to gawk at, but I'm uncomfortable.

After our meal, the server passes me the steak in a container and gives us the bill before picking up our plates and cutlery.

I open my purse, but Reaper pulls cash out of his wallet and places the money down next to the receipt. "I'll pay for mine." I reach for the receipt to see the cost, but he takes the receipt and cash and slides it over to his side.

"You don't pay when you're with me."

My mouth opens, but from the confident look on his face, I don't think I'll win this battle, so I slam my mouth shut. When we stand, he slides his hand in mine.

The ladies are loud when they talk.

"He's fine," one says.

"I'd let him do unimaginable things to me," another says, and they all cackle.

Reaper shifts to stand in front of me. Cupping my face in his hands and tilting my head up, he leans down and gives me a firm kiss. I gasp, and his tongue delves in, claiming me.

The women start cheering. One woman yells, "Go get it, girl!" making me pull back and laugh as those insecurities fall away.

AFTER OUR MOTORCYCLE RIDE AROUND THE COAST, WE RETURN home. He parks in the shed, and when I get off the motorcycle, I hand the helmet to Reaper. I wait for him, and we walk inside together. When we walk through the house, it's silent until everyone claps and someone wolf whistles.

My hands cover my mouth. Have I forgotten something? Is it Reaper's birthday?

Viper steps forward. "Is it official? Are Mommy and Daddy finally together?"

I laugh at my crazy family, then step over to Reaper. He bends down as I lean up on my toes, and he brings his lips to mine in a sweet, soft kiss. Everyone cheers again. The look of devotion in his eyes has me wanting to kiss him again, but I resist—*for now*.

Elena runs over to me with the biggest smile on her face and gives me a hug. "I'm so happy for you . . . and for me," she laughs. "I've got you back!"

She's the biggest sweetheart.

I wipe my eye. "I love you."

She pulls back. "Aww . . . are you crying?" She hugs me again, tighter this time. "I love you, too."

We have a small celebration with drinks, but Reaper and I leave early. Reaper walks into his room, but I pause by the door as I watch a woman follow Bomber into his. She has a short, fitted dress on, and I find it odd because I've never seen him with anyone before. After Bomber's door closes, I walk into Reaper's room and close the door behind me.

"I just saw a woman walk into Bomber's room," I mention as I get into bed and pull the duvet over me. Reaper gives me a quizzical look, so I keep going. "Elena said he's never with the sweet butts."

Reaper's mouth goes into a straight line, like he's trying not to laugh, but his eyes give him away. "What are you trying to say?"

"I thought he was celibate." I had no other explanation.

He barks out a chuckle, making his chest shake. "*No*, he's not celibate, far from it."

I shrug. "I don't know. He got angry when Grace touched him."

"You're correct. He doesn't sleep with sweet butts. The woman you saw going into his room is an escort."

My face scrunches. "Why would he pay for it when he can get it for free?"

"No attachments."

I frown, taking a moment to think before I respond. "He never wants to find a partner?"

"No."

"But why?"

He raises a brow and the corner of his lip curves. "Why do you want to know?"

"Surely, he doesn't really want to be alone forever, does he?" I'd like to think that finding that special someone could make him happy.

"It's his choice. He doesn't want to get involved, and for him, it's a transaction. He gets what he wants and there are no emotions, no commitment, just sex."

I raise my chin and shake my head.

He chuckles. "You see things differently. The societal norms. Nothing about us is normal. Don't try to understand the men in this MC because you most likely never will. Accept them for who they are."

"I do, but . . . Bomber seems so . . . I thought a woman could improve his mood."

Reaper's arm comes around me, pulling me into him. "Bomber is directly responsible for the club's security and safety. There's a story about why he is the way he is, but I can't share it with you. I can say that it contributed to why he takes his job seriously."

"It's bad, isn't it?" I ask.

"Our experiences shape who we are today. Every member of the MC has a story, and, yes, most of us have gone through a traumatic experience. Some people meet the devil and come back to earth still swinging."

I couldn't agree more. "I've met the devil." My shoulders slump. "His name is Beau."

"If he's the devil, I'd die to be cast to him, to show him exactly what hell is." Reaper's voice crackles with anger, a reminder of his darker side, the soldier who needs to protect everyone he cares about.

I sit up. "You know about my past. Can you tell me more about yours?"

Something flashes across his face, but I wasn't sure what it was. "What do you want to know?"

Excitement buzzes inside of me at getting to know Reaper. "I have so many, but let's start simple. Do you have any siblings?"

He slowly nods. "A sister."

"What about your parents? Do you still talk to them?"

"I don't know where they are. My last memory of them was when me and my sister were taken away from them and placed into foster care."

"I'm sorry," I reply, feeling bad for them.

He shrugs. "No need to be sorry. It was a long time ago, and we turned out fine."

"Do you talk to your foster parents?"

"No, but they weren't bad people. They did their best. Sherrie and Larry took on five foster kids of different ages. Sherrie worked two jobs and got money from the government for looking after us, and her partner, Larry, stayed home."

I pull my hair over my shoulder and rake my fingers through it as I think about what else to ask. "What made you want to join the army?"

He let out an exasperated sigh. "Everything."

"What do you mean by that?"

"Larry watched the news every night, and most of the time I watched it with him. Every day, they talked about violence, war, and terrorists, and as I got older, I wanted to help and do something about it."

I lean up and place a soft kiss on his cheek. "You're a good person."

His face goes blank, and a shiver racks my body. It was as if I saw his soul leave his eyes. "Don't get me confused and put me on a pedestal. I killed who they ordered me to kill. I never asked questions about who they were or what they had done."

A coldness solidifies his voice, and it makes me frown. I didn't mean to upset him. "You have a past, but my feelings about you won't change."

He looks away, and that familiar fire returns to my stomach. When I sit up, his eyes return. "Why don't you believe me?" I'm annoyed and saddened. "You risked your life to go to war for your country."

He sits up with his back against the headboard. His pained expression nearly levels me. "I've killed a woman before."

I pause, but he would not kill for no reason. "Why?"

He hangs his head, then rubs down his face, and the Reaper I know is back. I crawl over and straddle his legs. I grasp his face, feeling the prickles of his beard on my fingers. I lift his head to make him look at me. The torment in his eyes is palpable. I blink a few times, holding back tears; it hurts me to see him in pain, but I know it's my turn to be strong. "Please, share with me what happened."

His eyes close briefly before he speaks. "With all my training, nothing could have prepared me for war. Every day was death and destruction. But I'll never forget killing that young woman. She wore a coat that looked too big for her, and I thought she had a bomb under it." His voice cracks as sadness falls from his lips and regret fills his eyes.

Reaper's face blurs. "Why did she have a bomb strapped to her?"

"I'm not sure if she had one, but I heard stories of women

wearing them by choice but also because they could have been forced to. They used woman and children against us, knowing full well that we value their lives."

My chest constricts but I need to know more. I want him to share this burden with me, knowing how much better I felt when I told Elena about what I had gone through.

"What happened?"

He goes quiet, lost in thought, so I wait patiently for his response. "We were given information that a target was in an area close by. So we traveled there, and the men were going through each home, one by one, searching for him. When they came out of one home and were about to walk into another, the woman had come from the back of the house to the side and was moving toward them. She had a large coat on and . . ." He shakes his head and swallows. "I couldn't see a bomb, but I had seconds to react, so I shot her."

I kneel, wrap my arms around his shoulders and hold him tightly, his chest against mine as his arms snake around my back. The tears fall, and my emotions strangle me. I inch back and peer into Reaper's tortured eyes, and all I want to do is take his pain from him. Leaning forward, I kiss a tear falling down his cheek.

"Did you find out if she had a bomb on her?" I ask in a small voice.

He shakes his head. "We had a mission to complete."

"You had to make a tough decision, but it doesn't make you a bad person. Thank you for sharing your story with me."

I needed it as much as he needed to talk to someone. Seeing his vulnerability and hearing his struggles only makes me love him more.

I focus on his lips, then on his eyes.

I love him.

My body pulses with the need to kiss him. My hands seem

to move on their own accord, and I wrap my arms around his neck and pull his lips to mine. For a second, he pauses as if in shock but then relaxes and kisses me harder.

He coaxes my lips open, allowing his tongue access, then expertly massages it against mine. There's a hurricane of emotions inside me. He's the one for me. My arms tighten around his neck, increasing the passion of the kiss, causing my lips to plump under the assault. My body heats, but there's also an ache between my thighs that no kiss will fix, so I pull away, leaving him open-mouthed.

Lifting one leg over him, I crawl to the edge of the bed and step down. I grasp the edge of my dress and lift it over my head, then drop it on the floor by my feet. As his eyes admire my body, I've never felt so sexy, so I unclasp my bra and slide my arms out. A small moan escapes my lips in relief, and my nipples pebble from the cool air.

"I've been fantasizing over your body for a long time now, and every inch of you is perfect."

With the hunger in his eyes and his deep, hungry voice, I believe him. Tension coils from his body, like he wants to get up and touch me but he's forcing himself to stay seated.

My underwear is next, and I pull them down my ass and thighs, step out of them and to the bed, and crawl toward him.

"You're in control, baby."

My pulse thrashes against my skin. "Shirt off!"

He leans forward from the headboard, lifts his shirt over his head, then throws it to the side.

My teeth dig into my lower lip as my greedy eyes gaze at every ridge on his body. When my eyes reach his groin, his cock is straining against his jeans, so I reach for his belt and work on his button, my fingers fumbling, a mix of nerves and desire.

He takes over, pulling his zipper down, then brings his

jeans and briefs under his ass and down his legs, kicking them off when they get to his feet.

He's relinquishing all control, and I'm sure it's not easy for a man like him. I know I need it, but I will also take full advantage of it.

"No touching me until I say."

His jaw clenches, and his head falls back onto the head-board with a light thump. I wrap my hand around the base of his cock. His head whips up as he hisses through his teeth, and it makes me feel powerful. I grip him firmly and stroke his thick length again and again.

I shift closer and place my hand on his shoulder for lever-age. I tremble as I lift one leg over him to straddle him. He lifts his hands. "No touching," I say in a seductive voice, and he swears under his breath. My hand reaches between us, grabbing his shaft again, then I shift back so he's exactly where I want him to be. Inching down, I arch my back so he's at my opening.

He stretches me as I ever so slowly inch down further, but I hover there and grind on him, working only the tip, letting him feel how wet I am. The groan that comes from deep within his chest does crazy things to my insides, and I grind again, being careful not to go down any farther.

"Fuuuuck, Ava . . . You're torturing me! I need to touch you. Please let me touch you."

Reaper, an alpha male begging to touch me, only makes the ache between my thighs worse. "Okay," I whisper and welcome his touch. Without missing a beat, one hand tangles in my hair, and he crashes his lips to mine while the other is on my breast, kneading it. I moan when his thumb rubs against my nipple, but it's swallowed up by the kiss. Tongues collide as my body burns with need.

His lips leave mine and he places open-mouthed kisses on my throat and linger on my pulse point. His hand moves to my other breast, and he bends down, taking it into his mouth, making my head fall back as he swirls his tongue around my nipple.

The need is too strong, so I lower myself, inch by inch, down his cock, as deep as I can until it is buried to the hilt.

"Condom," he says through a ragged breath.

I raise myself and grind down. There's a mix of pleasure and anguish on his face. "I don't think I can get pregnant."

"Good. I want to feel you around me. Ride me, beautiful."

My insides lock onto him in bliss as I feel his hand on my hip, his mouth on my other breast, inducing a faint moan. As I arise, my arms tighten around his neck and I grind down, getting into a rhythm. A sheen of sweat covers my body, strands of hair sticking to my forehead.

My rhythm gets faster as the pressure keeps building, my body desperate for release. Reaper's thumb meets my clit, and I gasp at the sensation. He applies pressure and rubs circles. With a low cry, I break apart as my body clenches and shudders around him. Distantly, I hear him say my name as I struggle to catch my breath at the pleasure coming in waves. He lets out a guttural groan, and I collapse, my body leaning against his.

Once the haze fades, I realize something. "That's the first orgasm I've ever had with a partner."

TWELVE
KING REAPER

Reaper

I FEEL LIKE A KING.

I can't believe it was her first orgasm. I'm getting a hard-on just thinking about it. I'm thrilled she's back in my bed, where she belongs. The warmth of her body, the soft sound of her breathing, soothes something inside me. I relish the fact that she's finally *mine*.

Last night was incredible. She's lying on her side away from me, but when I lift the blanket, I can see the sexy curves of her hips and ass. I smile to myself. I'm a lucky son of a bitch. All I want to do is sink back into her.

My phone rings. I roll over and see the private investigator's number up on my screen. My stomach twists at the familiar feeling that something's wrong.

"Reaper speaking."

"Hi. I'm calling to update you. I've been staking out Beau's house for days, and he hasn't come home."

Dread washes over me. "Do you think he's planning something?"

"It's a possibility," he replies before a long pause. "I have covered cases like this before, and they don't end well."

I glance back at Ava, who's sleeping so soundly, and shake my head. "He dares comes near her, and he'll regret it."

"Once the victim has left a domestic violence relationship, that's when it's the most dangerous for them. I know she's safe with you, but keep that in mind because you don't know what state of mind that guy is in."

"I appreciate it. Can you stay there and do your best to search for him by any means necessary to find out where he is or where he's gone?"

"I'll keep you updated."

I white-knuckle the blanket. The beautiful woman in my bed has found her feet and is smiling again. The last thing I want to do is ruin that because of that oxygen thief.

Looking at my phone, I go through the contacts and call the club's attorney.

"Hi, Reaper,"

"What happens if Ava wants a divorce, but no one can locate Beau?"

"The judge will most likely rule in Ava's favor."

Rubbing my chin, I peer off. Well . . . that could work for everyone because that asshole will never hurt her again. Being in the military, I know how fragile life is, but being with Ava has shown me a whole new meaning. I've lost brothers, but I won't come back from losing her.

"Thanks. Bye."

Ava rolls over toward me with heavy eyes, her long auburn hair draping over her shoulder. "Good morning," she says in a husky voice.

"Good morning, beautiful."

She smiles but averts her eyes.

"What do I have to do or say to make you believe that you're beautiful?"

Her nose scrunches, but it gives me an idea.

"Are you ticklish?" I ask with a raised brow.

Her eyes narrow warily. "I am . . . Isn't everyone?"

She can't even lie, knowing it's to her detriment.

I jump up and roll her onto her back. She squeals in surprise. I grab her tiny hands and raise them above her head. Her bright-green eyes and mouth are wide, and it makes me give her a wicked smile while leaning over her. "Now say 'I'm beautiful.'"

Her head rocks from side to side. My free hand rises. She bucks as I slowly trail my fingers down her arm. Her breathing quickens as I get closer, then I gently dig my fingers into her side and her underarm. Her laugh is like music to my ears as she wiggles and bucks from side to side, still laughing.

"Okay, okay," she says through heavy breaths. She looks me in the eyes, looking so serious, and says, "Reaper, you're beautiful."

My hands go straight to her sensitive spots again, and she cackles in laughter while trying to get out of my hold. "My woman has a smart mouth on her!"

"Okay, fine!" she says louder. "I'm beautiful."

I smile from ear to ear. "That's more like it."

Her chest is heaving, and I can't help but admire her perfect tits. My head moves to her boob, and my tongue rolls around the tight pink nub. A small gasp escapes from her mouth. I take her mouth in mine and devour her. I'll never tire of this.

BREAKFAST WAS AMAZING AS ALWAYS, BUT AFTERWARD, WHEN Ava, Elena, and the sweet butts go to clean up, I call for a meeting in church.

I'm at the head of the table and observe the men. Viper as VP is on one side and Bomber as sergeant at arms is on the other. The other men follow around the table.

"It's time to decide Rage's fate, whether we will patch him in. All hands raise in agreement," I say as I raise my hand.

Around the table, everyone raises theirs with no hesitation. Rage has felt a part of this family since he arrived, but we have a process, and every prospect has to earn their right to wear the club's patches.

"Ava is my ol' lady, and I'll be getting her a property cut." I peer down at the table. "Cash, can you organize this?"

He nods his head sharply.

Axle chuckles, making me look at him. "Have you got something to say?"

"Elena told me Ava didn't like that she was wearing one, especially the term 'property of.'"

I frown. I didn't even think about that. "Ava's husband has gone missing. We need to be on high alert. Ava and Elena are not allowed to leave the compound."

"Why is Elena not allowed to leave?" Axle asks.

"I think he'll come for Ava, and I don't want to give him any leverage. It won't be forever, and we can review this at a later stage, but until I find out about Beau's whereabouts, I want the women to remain here under our protection."

"That's a good plan. Thanks, Pres," Axle replies. "Before Beau went into hiding, Elena told me he was sending her and her parents messages, threatening to kill himself if he doesn't see Ava."

"Did she tell him to get it over and done with already? Saves us the hassle."

Everyone's eyes fall on Demon, and from the amusement

on the men's faces, I'd say he said out loud what everyone else was thinking.

"Twitch, do whatever you have to. I need to find him."

Twitch gives me a salute.

"I need everyone to be vigilant. On a different note, everything is ready for the marijuana deliveries, but I'll be staying with Rage and Twitch, just in case Beau tries anything. Viper will be in charge." Viper's smug smile shows he will love that. "The Kings of Chaos MC will meet you by the road, at the end of our property, when a time has been confirmed."

Bomber leans closer. "Did you get a sense that something was different last time we went to their clubhouse?"

I think back to that day. My mind was on Ava. "I didn't notice anything. Why? Did you?"

Viper chimes in. "They were quieter than normal."

Bomber and Viper have the strongest instincts and intuition I have seen, and that is why they have the positions they do.

"The Kings of Chaos president couldn't even make eye contact when you were talking," Bomber says.

"I'm calling tomorrow off," I bark.

The room is silent. Everyone's staring at us.

Viper's hand goes to my shoulder. "We've got this, Pres. Delivery is due. We can't afford to piss anyone off. We'll get it done with no issues. You have our word."

My stomach twists knowing he's right and that I can't watch their back makes me anxious. "If anyone gets even the hint of suspicion about anything related to the Kings of Chaos, inform Viper immediately."

As we walk out of church, I move straight to the bar, open the fridge, and take a cold beer out. I twist the lid off and gulp down the refreshing liquid. It relieves none of the tension in my body. Ava stands by the dishwasher. When I make eye contact with her, she frowns at me.

She closes the dishwasher door and walks over to me. She takes the beer from my hand, and turns, putting it on the bar, then stands on her toes, draping her hands around the back of my neck. The hint of a smile crosses my lips, my arms going around her. Everything seems better when I'm holding her.

"Beau's gone missing. I've got a private investigator looking into him. We'll find him," I reassure her.

"I'm sorry," she says, then sighs. "I'm sorry, *again*. Beau is a nightmare that won't go away."

He sure is, but I pull her tighter.

"Never apologize for him. Do you know where he could be?"

"I wouldn't know. He never spent time with his family, and the only friends he spoke about were his colleagues, but he never saw them after he got fired. He mostly stayed at home."

In her eyes, I can see that she's scared. "I'll be here for you, to protect you, so try not to worry."

"I know . . . and I'd be happy to never hear his name again." She peers off before looking at me again with a seductive grin, and all my problems vanish.

The only thing left is her. She pulls away but puts her delicate hand in mine, lacing our fingers and stepping forward. Tugging on my hand, she gestures for me to follow her. Over her shoulder, she gives me a suggestive eyebrow raise, and that's all it takes to get my dick hard.

We hurry through the clubhouse and up the stairs. I stop until she turns around and looks at me, then I pick her up. She shrieks, her legs wrapping around my waist.

"Put me down. I'm too heavy."

I laugh at her ridiculous comment. When I get to *our* bedroom door, I open it, step inside, then kick it shut with my foot. I move to the bed and gently pull her arms from my neck and push her onto the bed. She bounces slightly on the mattress.

"You're my fantasy." I lean down over her, with one hand supporting my weight, while the other cups her tit through her bra. I enjoy her little gasp.

"These are the best tits I've seen in my life, and this . . ." My hands move to her side and travel down her body to her thigh. "Perfect curves, round ass, and creamy skin. I'll never get enough of you."

Heat flares in her eyes. "Kiss me." Her voice is a breathy plea.

My mouth collides with hers. She tastes sweet, but her tongue is desperate and wild, which increases the ache deep in my groin. There's a tug on my belt, but I pause and inch back, in case she changes her mind.

"Reaper," she pleads, "get your pants off. Now!"

The sassy comment is the approval I needed, so I lever myself off her body and make work of my jeans as she undoes hers. After I kick them off my feet, I slide my arms out of my cut, placing it on the ground, followed by my shirt. I watch on, enthralled, when she takes her bra off and throws it to the side. She then spreads her legs wide, welcoming me.

An animalistic growl sounds low in my throat. My eyes travel up her body. While appreciating every curve, I stroke myself. Ava's tongue pokes out of her mouth, sweeping across her bottom lip as she watches me, like she's starving. I step toward the bed and slowly moved up her body, watching her chest rise and fall.

I slide my hand from her smooth belly to her breasts, and she shivers from my touch. Her skin is warm and soft. Her hand moves between us, and she grips my cock, gliding it between her folds and onto her clit. My eyes roll back.

Thank fuck for no condoms—but only with her have I never worn one.

Gripping her hips, I position myself at her entrance, then press inside inch by aching inch. Our gazes lock, and the intimate connection is intense. I lean down and my mouth finds hers again, my tongue sinking inside her mouth. When her legs wrap around me, I rock my hips, thrusting in and out, slowly at first. There's a pinch of pain in my back from her nails sinking in.

Breaking the kiss, I look down. Her eyelashes flutter as she writhes underneath me.

"Harder," she begs, digging her heels into my ass.

I slam my hips against hers, releasing a cry of pleasure from her throat. Sweat drips from my skin as her muscles tighten around me. Her moans get louder as my pace gets faster. My dick pulses with the need to come.

Reaching between us, I rub her clit. She jerks when I press harder. Ava's teetering on the edge, but I didn't wait for her to come. Instead, I keep pounding into her, and she explodes like a goddess, screaming my name. I thrust two more times and follow her over the edge.

I jolt awake. My eyes shoot open as I gasp for air. I rub my eyes. The room is dark. Ava stirs in my arms. "Shhh," I whisper, and she snuggles in, falling back asleep.

The nightmare I just had, of Beau taking her, was one of the worst I've had. It used to be the flashbacks of war that haunted me every night. The screams of men, the explosions, the gunshots. It never ended until Ava spent the night in my bed and silenced those demons. But now that there's a potential threat to her life, those nightmares have changed to losing her.

Most of the men have PTSD, but that's the consequences

we bear from going to war. I'll never regret going because of my brothers I have saved and protected and the targets I've eliminated to protect our country, like I'll never regret protecting Ava.

I lean in closer to her, breathing in her sweet vanilla scent, listening to her breathing. She's with me, and she's safe. This powerful pull urges me to go into sniper mode and hunt Beau down, but I can't bring myself to leave her side.

THIRTEEN
THE PERFECT STORM

Ava

"We've got to make a delivery tonight with the Kings of Chaos," Reaper says from beside me. He's sitting up, leaning against the headboard.

I pull my hair over my shoulder as I keep braiding it, wondering whether I should talk to him about it. "Are you allowed to tell me what that means?"

"You can ask me anything. We grow and distribute marijuana."

Relieved, I blink a few times. I can live with that. "Where do you grow it?"

"Further up the mountain, past the cabin."

His honesty is always refreshing.

"Why do you need the other MC? Don't you have enough men?"

"They have chapters around the country, so they are one of our biggest customers. Their MC provides additional protection until we unload, then they distribute it between themselves."

Everything makes sense now.

"I'm going to miss you."

"No!" He stares at me with a weird look on his face. "I'm staying here with you."

I'm torn. I selfishly want him to stay, but he wants to go.

He leans down and kisses my forehead. "We have done this many times before. The men will be fine without me."

The dark circles under his eyes say otherwise.

"Have you slept?"

The touch of a smile graces his lips. "Don't you worry about me."

I frown. "I'm not *that* girl. I don't want to force you to choose between me and your men."

"*You're* not making me choose. I want to stay here with you."

He sounds sincere, but I still feel like he's being forced to choose.

"Well, I'll go with you on the ride. Then you won't—"

"Not a chance in hell."

"Why?"

He shakes his head. "I want you *away* from the danger."

"You don't need to babysit me. No one has seen Beau, and it's not like he has any close friends. He wouldn't be able to go against anyone in your club, so if Rage and Twitch are staying, then I'll be fine."

He cracks his neck to the side. Any time Beau's name is brought up in conversation, a tension radiates from Reaper's body, and I don't blame him.

"Twitch and the private investigator have been spending every day looking for him, so until I know his exact location, I'm not leaving your side."

I attempt to smile because I am grateful, but the guilt still eats at me. "It means a lot that you have organized all of that. I have noticed there's always at least one man in the computer room, watching the cameras." I wish I could help. My face brightens. "I'll have to make something extra good for the men for dinner to say thank you."

"Believe me, they appreciate every meal you cook for them. It's not that I don't think the men can do the delivery without me. I'm struggling with letting go of control because this will be the first time I don't have their back."

My lips curve into a cheeky grin. "You don't struggle to let go of control when it comes to me."

He swiftly moves and leans over me, pushing me down onto my back. His lips are so close to mine I can breathe in the air he breathes out. "You're different," he says, then kisses me.

I LIFT THE CUP OF COFFEE TO MY LIPS AND HAVE A SIP OF THE HOT drink as I watch Reaper pace in the kitchen. It's unsettling.

Elena is sitting next to me with her elbows on the kitchen counter and her head in her hands. She mindlessly stares at the wall. They are quiet, but I can see the worry in their eyes. I was asleep when the men left late last night. Conan barks again.

"What's wrong with Conan lately?" Elena asks. "He's been barking more, and he's getting worse. It's at all hours too."

I've noticed, but I don't believe he barks at nothing. "Maybe he's been seeing more wildlife than normal."

A phone rings, interrupting our conversation. Reaper swiftly grasps his phone from the counter.

"Reaper," he answers on the second ring. I can hear the

hum of a voice but not what is being said. "What do you mean Jude isn't there? No, he didn't tell me." Reaper nods. "Okay, okay." His body relaxes, so I gather everyone and everything is okay. "I knew you would be fine without me, but I don't enjoy being left here. How long until you will be back?" He looks to Elena, who's leaning forward toward him, watching his every move.

"Can you put Axle on for me?" Elena sits up taller, her eyes widen, and her hand comes out for the phone.

"You should appreciate your wife." There's a pause. "Because I'm here, and the whole time, she's been worrying about you." Elena smirks at Reaper. "Here, I'll put her on." He hands the phone to Elena.

"Babe! Please tell me you will be home soon." She sighs. "Good." She breathes out a gush of air. "Can you please take Reaper with you next time?"

Reaper gives Elena a puzzled expression. There's laughter through the phone.

Elena looks Reaper dead in the eyes when she says, "He's been stressing out, which has made me stress more!" There's laughter again while Reaper shakes his head. "Okay, babe. Love you. Bye." She hands the phone back to Reaper.

He takes it and crosses his arms. "I haven't been stressed."

I glance at Elena, and we both quirk an eyebrow at him.

These two stress heads can sit and watch the clock together. "I'm going outside to play with Conan."

As I move through the back of the clubhouse and out the back door, I scan the yard for Conan, but I can't see him.

"Conan," I yell as I search again. Barking is coming from the front, so I trail around the side and make my way to the front to see him standing like a statue with his ears erect. He barks again.

"Hey," I call out, and his head whips to me. Instantly, his ears drop, his tail wags, and he runs over. When he reaches me, I pat him. "We need to have a serious conversation. You have to calm the barking down. People are starting to whine."

His head tilts, though I'm sure he has no idea what I'm talking about.

Motorcycles rev in the distance. My first thought is, *Wow, the men were quick.*

Conan barks and bolts toward the gate. I groan at having to walk down the driveway. "Conan!" I don't know what's gotten him so on edge lately.

I squint at the men. I don't recognize them. Considering the Kings of Chaos are out of town as well, it's most likely people I don't know. Conan isn't fond of strangers, so I run to him, then pull on his collar.

"C'mon, out the back. Let's go."

As the motorcycles get closer, my heart becomes frantic.

"Out the back now!" My voice is louder and stern. Conan looks up at me, and I point to the backyard. He follows as we make our way to the house.

As the motorcycles get to the gate, I glance back once more. I swear the men are from the Kings of Chaos.

I take Conan through the house because I'm not sure whether the men were going to come inside or out the back. Rage meets us at the front door, then smiles at Conan, patting him on the head. "Hello, boofhead." He glances at me, then over my shoulder. "Are the men here already?"

"No, but I swear it's the Kings of Chaos."

He gives me a weird look as Elena rushes toward us. "It's not Axle," I tell her, knowing who she is keenly waiting for. She stops and glances at me with a deflated look before turning and walking away.

Rage turns swiftly and walks toward the computer room, so I follow in curiosity. When we enter, Twitch and Reaper are looking at the screen that shows the front of the house, but it's zoomed in toward the gate.

"I didn't expect them here," Reaper says, and an unsettled feeling takes root in my stomach.

Twitch looks up at Reaper from his seat. "Do you want me to let them in?"

He pauses. "Not yet."

"What's Jude doing with them?" Rage asks.

"I don't know, but let's find out."

Twitch nods and presses the intercom. "Hey, Jude, what are you doing here?"

Jude chuckles. "I decided to come up and have a beer."

Reaper leans down and presses the intercom button. "Viper mentioned you weren't with your men during delivery."

"That's what I came here to discuss."

All eyes are on Reaper as we wait for his decision, but he turns to Rage. "Call the men now. It's only a precaution but tell them to be on alert. Jude is here with two men I don't know, and that prospect is with him, the one I told him to get rid of."

Rage pulls out his phone and walks out of the room.

"Have you got your gun on you?" Reaper asks Twitch.

His question makes my stomach sink. Twitch pulls a gun from under the computer table.

"Are you going to let us in? I'm desperate for a cold beer," Jude says.

Reaper shakes his head.

"Maybe another time," Twitch replies.

One man we don't know gets something out of his backpack, and as he walks toward the gate, the others reverse. "What are they doing?"

An explosion makes me take a few steps back. There are also distant screams, which I presume are from the sweet butts. I release a shaky breath as I get my bearings. Conan's barking, but I've got hold of his collar.

Reaper swiftly moves to me. "Go upstairs and grab my spare gun. It's in the top drawer of my cabinet."

The monitor shows a plume of smoke, and the men walk through the entrance with their guns drawn.

Reaper squeezes my shoulder, and I blink a few times. "Did you hear me?"

My heart is in my throat, but I nod. "I've shown you how to use it, and there are already bullets in it. Take Conan with you and find Elena."

The mention of Elena's name changes me from a state of shock to focus. She's depending on me, and I need to keep myself together.

Rage runs in the room. Reaper looks at him. "Go get the keys to the truck and go with them. We will force them away from the driveway to give you safe passage."

Rage leaves immediately.

"No!" I yell. Reaper can shoot well, but it didn't matter. There were four men and only two if Rage plays bodyguard. "You need Rage with you. We will be fine."

My eyes flick back to the screen, and the men are getting closer to the house.

Rage returns and stands by the door, waiting for me.

"There's no time. I need you to go now! Rage, give her your gun and get the sweet butts upstairs first."

Cracks of gunshots hit the clubhouse, making me scream. Conan is barking, going ballistic. I turn to my name being yelled. It's Rage.

"Go," Reaper yells at us. I give Reaper one more look over my shoulder. He must see my hesitation because he points to the exit. "Please, I need you safe."

I reluctantly turn and follow Rage.

Elena is at the bottom of the stairs. Tears stream down her cheeks as she talks on the phone, her hand shaking. "Who is here?"

When we reach her, we all stand against the wall. Rage takes the phone from her hand and brings it to his ear. "Axle, we need you now! Jude is here, shooting at us." He hangs up and gives Elena her phone, takes Conan's collar from me, and peers at Elena. "You need to take Conan while Ava takes my gun." Elena swallows hard, then grasps Conan's collar. Conan pulls forward, like he wants to run after the men shooting at us, but Elena holds her ground, pulling back on his collar.

"Hold these," he says and places the car keys in my hand. He reaches down, pulls out his gun, and passes it to me.

I stare at the cold metal object in my hand. I never wanted to use this.

"Stay here. If anyone comes through the back door, shoot them!" Rage runs through the house.

The gunshots are loud cracks, one after another, but then I hear the shattering of glass. With all the commotion, from the screaming to the bullets and to Conan barking, all I can think about is Reaper.

Rage returns to us, the sweet butts behind him. They are crying, their hands covering their faces.

"Upstairs," he yells to them. They quickly dart up, following his instructions.

My heart constricts more and more with every gunshot. *I can't lose Reaper.*

I turn to Elena. "We are getting out of here now."

She looks at me questioningly. "But Rage said . . ."

"The men need all the help they can get. Now come on before he gets back!"

I shove the keys in my pocket, then place both hands on the gun. Elena grabs my shirt, and we all move swiftly through the house. "Get farther back."

We reach the back door. I open it an inch and peek out. When I see no one, I push it open farther and slowly walk outside, scanning every inch of the backyard.

"It's clear."

My heart pounds. Rage will be here any moment, so when Elena and Conan meet me, I rush to the side of the clubhouse. I draw my gun as I check again, but like Reaper said, he would be forcing them away from us. The gunshots sound farther away than they did before.

I turn to Elena and pull the keys out of my pocket. "The truck is there. Run with me!" I press the fob and the lights of the truck flash, then we sprint toward it. "Get in!" I open the back door for Conan.

He jumps up with no hesitation. I shut the door and jump in the front seat, place the gun in the center console, then put the key in the ignition.

Elena puts her seatbelt on. She stares ahead with big eyes. I put the car in drive and take off. When we leave down the driveway, I look in the rearview mirror to see Rage with his arms up in the air. I frown, but I'm convinced I made the right decision. I floor the gas pedal, and more dirt kicks up behind us.

Elena's phone rings. She pulls it out of her pocket. I glance to see Axle's name on the screen. She brings it to her ear. "Hey, I'm with Ava. We drove away. How long are you going to be?" With frantic breaths, she pauses, listening to his response. "Yes, we are okay. Thirty minutes? Please hurry. They need you. Be safe. I love you, too."

We travel the dirt road, driving past the warehouse. "Thirty minutes seems so long."

I don't get to hear her answer because a car comes from the right, crashing into us with a *thwack* and the tearing of metal on metal.

FOURTEEN

I'D DIE FOR YOU

Ava

I slowly blink a few times. My body is heavy. I'm hunched over in my seat. My head's throbbing, with a warm trickle of liquid oozing down my face. I touch my head and peek down at my hand to see bright-red blood.

My head turns. "Elena."

My voice comes out, but it's barely audible. She's leaning off to the side closest to me with her hair covering her face. "Elena," I say, panicked. I grab her shoulder and shake it. She doesn't answer and my heart skyrockets. Tears burn my eyes. A whine in the backseat makes me think Conan is alive . . . for now.

I undo my seatbelt. When I turn to Elena's side, I lean over to check her pulse and hear a car door shut. I turn my head and suddenly I can't breathe. I frantically search for the gun or Elena's phone. I scan under my legs, then over to Elena's. The gun is by her foot.

As I lean down my door opens. Beau stands next to me,

staring with wild eyes. "Get out of the car," he says in a feral snarl.

I don't answer straight away, considering my options. Rage or Reaper could be here any moment now. Conan's growl rumbles from the back, making me wonder if he can move.

"NO!" I scream back at Beau.

His eyes widen, his stare hardening. He reaches for me, but I shove him away. He keeps trying, but so do I. I shove, slap, then I turn my leg and try to kick him away while Conan barks. Beau's arm goes to his waist and he pulls out a gun. I gasp.

I slowly put my hands up in surrender. "Okay . . . I'm getting out."

I turn and put both feet on the ground, my legs shaking as I stand. My head spins, but I keep myself upright.

Conan's deep, constant barks make Beau turn and aim his gun at the back seat. I leap, taking two steps over to stand in front of the back door, in front of Conan.

Beau glares. "You'd protect a dog but make an idiot out of me?"

His breathing is heavy, his eyes showcasing dark circles.

"Ava," I hear softly from the front seat.

"Take me," I blurt out to Beau, not wanting to draw any attention to Elena. "You came here for me. Now what?"

His head cocks an inch to the side. "We're going for a drive." He grabs the top of my arm, his grip painful. I don't fight. I want Elena and Conan safe. "Where are we driving to?" I ask loudly, hoping Elena can hear.

He mumbles to himself as we walk to his car but then stops, and as soon as I see that hostile look in his eyes, I know what's coming because I'd seen it once before.

I feel a stinging pain between my eyes, and the force of the blow makes me fall. My head throbs as I taste copper in my mouth. Everything is off center. I can't see straight. He grips my arm and then I'm being pulled to my feet, toward the car, though I keep stumbling.

He pushes my head down and I fall into a familiar seat. My eyesight slowly levels out while the driver's side door shuts. The car starts, but it makes a winding sound. His hands slam on the steering wheel, making me jolt. He tries it again, and it turns over and starts, though it backfires and the engine is louder than normal. A familiar beep signals the lock on the doors. As he reverses slowly, metal screeches as the vehicles pull away from each other.

I'm on the edge of my seat, my eyes scanning Elena. The side windshield has shattered, and there are patches of blood on her arm.

Her head turns our way and she blinks, but she looks disoriented. Her mouth moves, but I can't understand what she's saying because the motor is loud. Worry slices through me. I hurt Beau's pride, so he may still stop to hurt her. He doesn't, though; he keeps driving, and at least knowing Beau won't hurt them provides a small bit of relief. I hope the men get to them in time.

My heart is heavy because I never told Reaper I love him. In a short period, he's shown me more about life and love than anybody I've met. He's become my sanctuary. Being with him has allowed me to finally feel safe, secure, and at peace with who I am and what I want in a partner. The thought of never seeing him again fills me with terror. We needed more time. I turn my head to look out the window as I try to hide my tears.

"What are you crying about?" The disgust in his voice is unmistakable. "Your dog, your sister, or that criminal? I should be the one upset." He takes one hand off the steering wheel and points to his chest. "Me, not you! Me!" he screams.

His eyes return to the road, but his hands clench the

steering wheel. "Where are we going? You know the other men from the MC will be back soon. So just leave me here, and you will have enough time to escape."

He veers off to the side onto an overgrown dirt road. "If I can't have you, then no one can."

I look down at my hands tightly folded together. I loosen them and focus on my escape. I subtly move my legs to the side to see if there's a weapon or anything by my feet, but there's nothing. Then to the center console—nothing. I remember there being only registration papers in the glove compartment.

The car rocks as it travels over the rough ground.

"I gave you everything."

My eyes dart back to him. I bite back my reply because I know it wouldn't help me, but I can feel that burn of anger. I shove it down. "I know you did," I reply in the fake loving voice I know all too well.

"Then, why did you leave me? You had everything. You didn't work. I stayed with you, even though you couldn't get pregnant."

I flinch at the pregnancy taunt. It always wounded me when he mentioned it.

I clear my throat and sit up straighter in my seat. "I panicked."

His face scrunches as he glances at me, then his gaze returns to the road. "It was your fault! If you didn't carry on the way you did sometimes, maybe I wouldn't have gotten angry."

My jaw clenches, my knuckles white, as I hold my emotions in. I wait and try to breathe out some of the tension. "I'm sorry." I'm proud of how calm my voice sounds.

"It's too late now!"

I knew this when I looked into his cold, dead eyes. He came here to kill me. I try focusing again. If his gun is back in his holster, I could try to go for it. But he's much too strong for me to overpower him.

The steep mountain forces me to slide farther back into my seat. The car jolts forward, once, twice, then stops. Hope releases some of the pressure from my chest as I watch him turn the ignition over from the corner of my eye, but nothing happens.

"FUCK!" Beau screams and slams his hands on the steering wheel, startling me.

Now that the car is off, there's the sound of another car in the distance, and I pray that it's Reaper. Beau whips his head to see out the back window of the car. The beep signals the car's unlocked.

He pulls out his gun and aims it at me. He slowly opens his door and gets out. He rushes around the front of the car and to my side. I grip the door handle. There's tension on the other side of the door as he pulls it, but I lean back, gripping the door with everything I have. He bangs on the window, but the sound of the car is getting closer. If I can just hold on . . .

Glass shatters over my skin. My ears ring as he yanks the door open. I'm being pulled out to my feet. I search around my body, expecting to have been shot, but there are no wounds, only a couple of small specks of blood from the glass.

He tugs my arm hard again as the familiar MC van stops, with Reaper in the driver's seat, his eyes trained on us.

"Get out slowly!" Beau yells. "I'll kill her if you do anything stupid!"

The door opens and Reaper gets out. His muscles tense as he walks toward us. My eyes scan every inch of him. I can't see any injuries.

"Not any closer!" Beau warns as he shoves the cold gun

hard into my temple, making my eyes close briefly as he forces my head to move an inch to the side.

Reaper is still, but a vein is popping out in his neck.

"I know you've got a gun. Slowly, put it on the ground." Reaper's hand goes to his holster, but Beau yells. "I said slowly!" Reaper follows his command and grabs his gun. "Now, throw it away."

Reaper obeys. My mouth goes dry and my anxiety skyrockets. Reaper raises both hands in surrender and takes two steps closer to us.

"I said don't move," Beau booms, but motorcycles echo in the air, distracting Beau as he peers behind Reaper.

Reaper launches himself at Beau, but not before another piercing sound rings out. Blood drains from my face, leaving it cold. Within seconds, Reaper disarms Beau and headbutts him, making him fall. Reaper stands over him, aiming Beau's own gun at him. Then another gunshot cracks in the air, blending with loud motorcycles and a scream.

Beau's arm bleeds.

Reaper puts the gun in his holster and steps toward me. His eyes scan my face and body, then he pulls me into his chest. The tears come quickly as I melt into him. My arms are around him and I'm clinging to him like he might disappear.

"I've got you. You're safe now." He tenderly kisses the top of my head.

My arms only hold him tighter. His scent, and his warmth, engulfs me. Being in his arms is my happy place, my home.

"I thought I'd never see you again."

His lips curve up into a sexy smile. There's a cold sensation on my shoulder but then a thought comes to mind, so I pull back.

"Did you see Elena and Conan?" I ask, struggling to draw air into my lungs. "Are they okay? Are they alive?"

"Pres, is everything all right?" Viper says from beside us, gun in hand.

"We have a doctor and a vet on the way to the clubhouse. They should be there soon. Axle and Rage pulled them both from the car, mostly superficial injuries, but Conan might have a broken leg," Bomber answers me.

A weight lifts from my chest. "Thank you."

When I peer down at my shoulder, it's still cool, but it's wet and red. I gasp. *It's blood!* I lift my shirt a little to see under it, but there's no wound.

"You've been shot!" Bomber says.

Horror widens my eyes when I look up at Reaper, blood oozing from between his heart and shoulder, soaking his shirt.

Panic shoots through me as Viper says, "I'll call the doc."

Reaper takes his shirt off, but I snatch it from him and apply pressure to the wound.

"You shouldn't have done that," I say to him as guilt takes a hold of my throat. Tears fall.

"I've been through worse." His hand clasps the side of my face, and I lean into it. "As long as you're okay."

"Fucking lowlife scum!"

I turn to see Demon bend down and punch Beau in the face.

He stands and smiles his evil smile. "That's more like it!" Then he looks to Reaper with a raised brow. "I thought you were a perfect shot."

"I am, but I didn't want him to bleed out . . ."

My eyes bounce between the two, confused.

Demon's grin spreads and excitement flashes in his eyes. He looks back at Beau. "Oh, we're going to have some fun with you."

His voice is unnerving. I think I know what he means, but that thought goes to the back of my head. All I care about is

Reaper right now. I feel a coolness in my hand, so I glance up to see blood soaking through Reaper's shirt.

"Reaper needs the doc now!" I cry out.

"I'll get Rage to bring the other van back so him and Demon can pick up this piece of shit," Viper says as he tilts his head in Beau's direction.

Reaper sways and takes a step forward but falls. A scream tears from my mouth, but Bomber and Viper are on either side of him, holding him upright. They move briskly to the van, and I follow them.

Bomber opens the back door. "Ava, you go in first."

I step up and move to the back. Then Bomber and Viper lifts Reaper inside and places him on the ground in front of me. Bomber takes his shirt off and applies pressure to Reaper's wound as Viper rushes out of the van, slams the door shut, hurries to the driver's side, and gets in. The van starts and I hear Viper on the phone, but I'm too focused on Reaper's face draining of all color.

I sit on the ground and gently lift Reaper's head, shuffle forward, and put his head on my lap. One of my tears falls on his cheek and runs down his face. I gently wipe it, feeling the prickles of hair on my finger. "I love you. I love you so much." I lean down closer to him. "Please wake up," I whisper. "We haven't had enough time together. I want my happy ever after with you."

There's a touch on my back, and I look up to see Bomber. "He's strong."

The sadness that cuts into his tone only makes my tears fall faster. It's a reminder that everyone loves Reaper and that we are all struggling to see him like this.

I gaze at Bomber's hand, where the blood has seeped through the shirt. I gasp. "But that is so much blood."

Bomber doesn't reply. He's not one to lie and say everything will be okay when it may not be. Time goes by slowly while we travel back to the house. Every minute feels like an hour. My skin is hot and I'm flustered. The van jolts and skids on the driveway, and the back door flies open. I squint from the sun beaming into the van.

A woman and Twitch are behind the door, and I watch helplessly as Bomber and Twitch carry Reaper out. I get up and walk on shaky legs through the van.

"Ava!" Elena yells. As I step out of the van, she rushes over to me with one arm bandaged. We embrace each other. "I don't know what I'd do without you," she sobs.

My arms tighten around her as the tears fall again, making my eyes burn. I might be okay, but Reaper's not. I pat her back and try to pull away. "I'm sorry, I have to be with Reaper."

She lets go of me and hastily wipes her tears. We dash inside the clubhouse together.

"Where are they?" I ask as I desperately scan the house, but I see only the sweet butts standing by the bottom of the stairs.

"Ava!" Candy yells. They turn their heads, then rush to me. "I'm so glad you're okay."

I try to muster up some energy to give her a polite smile. Mercedez pats my back, and I see their eyes are red from crying. "Are all of you okay?" I look them over for injuries.

Candy's eyes widen, then she gives me a genuine smile. "We are. Thank you for asking." Then she peers up the stairs. "They set everything up in Reaper's room, ready for him for when he arrives. The men are up there."

I sniffle and try to hold myself together. "Thanks, girls." The adrenaline courses through me as I silently pray, *Please be alive.*

Elena and I dart up the stairs. As I walk through the hallway, I see Axle walking to us with his arms open, so I run to him. "Have you heard anything?"

My voice was raw and hoarse from crying. I know little time has passed, but my anxiety is making me feel physically sick. I want to see him, touch him, and tell him I'm here. He needs to fight . . . fight to come back to me.

Axle frowns. "Not yet. It might take a while. The bullet didn't go all the way through, so doc has to get it out and stop the bleeding, but that's only if there're no complications."

My legs collapse from underneath me, but Axle catches me. His arms hold me tight but his words shred my heart, and a sob tears from my throat from the agony assaulting me.

"It's my fault." I struggle to keep my voice even.

"No. It's Beau's," he reassures me. "He shot Reaper."

"Because of me!" My voice carries through the hallway.

He pulls back to make eye contact. "We were well aware of the risks of you staying here. Reaper protects people he cares about, at any cost. Even if it puts him in the firing line, it's who he is."

I know that, but the guilt still has a firm grip around my neck. My feet find the floor, and I stand upright and step out of his hold. I move toward Reaper's door. Bomber and Cash are leaning against the wall with their heads bowed, and Viper is sitting on the floor.

He looks up at me. "Don't blame yourself. None of us do."

Unfortunately, his kind words don't make a difference. Because I do blame myself. There's an eerie silence as we wait. The minutes blend, and I don't know how much time has passed.

Demon and Rage meet us. When I see that their hair is wet and they have showered, I stare at my red-stained hands and another sob rips out of my mouth. My tortured soul is in pure agony.

"Go have a shower. If anything happens, I'll come and get you," Elena says softly from beside me.

I need a shower, but I can't leave him, not even for a minute. "No." I glance at Bomber and Viper, who also haven't had showers.

The door opens and I step toward it, holding my breath. Viper stands, and we all wait for the doctor to speak.

She scans us. When her eyes land on me, she says, "I've stopped the bleeding and cleaned the wound. Because of the location of where the bullet is lodged, I'm unable to remove it."

Worry widens my eyes. "So you're leaving the bullet inside of him?" I ask, dumbfounded.

Her shoulders fall an inch. "Yes, I don't have all the surgical equipment here, and even if I did, removing the bullet can cause additional health issues and damage. In my medical opinion, it's not worth the risk."

I turn to Bomber. "Do we need to get a second opinion?"

She snorts, but I don't know her, and I want the best for Reaper.

Bomber's lip twitches as he looks at her and back at me. "Ava, meet Milly . . . Reaper's sister." He looks at her. "Milly, this is Reaper's woman, Ava."

My stomach sinks at how rude I was. I turn to apologize, but a smile has brightened up her face.

She leans in like she wants to hug me but stops when she looks at my clothes and hands. "It's a shame my brother didn't introduce us under better circumstances, but I can't tell you how happy I am that he's found someone."

The sincerity in her voice has me holding back tears, but I blink them back.

"We will need to talk later," she whispers to me, then looks around to everyone again. "He should wake up within the next few hours."

"Can I see him?" I blurt out. There's this desperate need to check for myself that he's alive.

Her hand comes out onto my arm. "Go have a shower. He's okay," she says slowly. "Then you can spend as much time as you want with him."

I suck in a sharp breath. Every part of me silently screaming *no*. An arm comes around my shoulders, and I look to see Elena.

"Come on, I'll get your clothes ready, and you can come straight back."

Milly gives me a reassuring smile. "He's going to be out of it for a while. You're not missing out on anything."

"O-kay," I answer reluctantly and walk toward the bathroom.

After I scrub my hands and arms of Reaper's blood and finish my quick shower, I get changed into the clothes Elena left and run into Reaper's room. The men are all stationed around him, except Bomber and Viper, who I assume have left to have showers too. As I step toward the end of the bed, I see Reaper still sleeping.

"Has he woken up yet?" I ask no one in particular.

"Not yet," Twitch answers. "I think he's been waiting for you."

At first I smile, but then my eyes narrow. "Where have you been?" All the men were here, except him. I want an explanation.

Axle chuckles. "She's onto you," he says to Twitch.

"I was here," he responds quickly. "Helping Milly during the operation."

"Yeah, because you want to bang her. You've got a death wish, I'm sure of it."

The men are laughing when Milly walks into the room.

"Shut the fuck up, Axle," Twitch grits between his teeth as the men laugh harder.

I shake my head at them and move to Reaper's side. I

crawl over to him on the bed. Bomber walks into the room, his eyes going straight to Reaper, then me.

"Everyone downstairs. Give Ava some time alone with Reaper. Milly, come and get us once he wakes up."

When it's only Bomber remaining, I say, "Thank you." He turns and gives me a small nod before he leaves.

Milly sits next to me on the bed. "Before you lie down, let me look at you. I'm not having Reaper wake up and then curse at me for not looking after his ol' lady."

A touch of a smile graces my lips because I can imagine him doing that. I shift in the bed to face her.

Her eyes travel around my face. Her hand comes to my nose and she feels it, making me flinch. "It's not broken." Her hands go to my arm, and she brings it toward her as her eyes study it. "Superficial cuts. Are you injured anywhere else?"

"No."

She raises her arm toward Reaper. "I won't stop you any longer. You can lie with him now."

I shuffle over and lie beside him. I briefly close my eyes, appreciating the warmth of Reaper's skin against mine. His face is still a little pale, but it is better than what it was.

I feel his sister's eyes on us. "He's the best person I know," she says, and when I peer at her, she's wiping the corner of her eye. "I told you before, but I'm so grateful he's found someone to love."

"Do you two have a close relationship?"

She smiles sincerely and stares off as if remembering the past. "I couldn't have wished for a better brother. Even when he was at war, he always sent me as much money as he could to help me pay for university. I got a scholarship, but I wouldn't have been able to afford it without Reaper. He has always had my back, no matter what."

I smile as my eyes drift back to Reaper, then to Milly.

"That sounds like him. Always doing everything he can for everyone around him."

"Keep going with the compliments," a gravelly voice says next to me.

Milly laughs as I shriek, "You're awake!"

The guilt hits me as I lean over, making sure I put no weight on him and press my lips to his. When I lean back, I say, "I'm so sorry you got shot." But then frustration washes over me. "Why did you do that? Put yourself in harm's way. I was so worried that I didn't get the chance to tell you I love you, and I do, Bain White. I love you so much." I press my lips to his again. I feel his smile against my lips, accompanied by a deep throaty chuckle.

"I love you, too, beautiful."

FIFTEEN
MC FAMILY

Six Weeks Later

Reaper

I lift my shirt and inspect the dark pink scar from the gunshot wound. It's still tender, but I've healed well. I'd do it again if it meant protecting Ava. To see how easily she fits in and genuinely looks after and cares for the men only makes me love her more.

As I pull the shirt over my chest, my phone rings. It's the attorney, but that can wait. I'm sure she's calling to update us on how the divorce is going. It's unfortunate that the process will take a lot longer since they cannot locate Beau. I chuckle to myself, knowing that they will never find him.

I've been waiting for Ava to ask me what happened to him, but she hasn't. Deep down, she probably knows but doesn't want to acknowledge it. I put my arms through my cut, walk over to the bathroom, and spray on the cologne Ava loves. When I walk out, I put my phone in my pocket, stride through the hallway, and step down the stairs but stop at the bottom when I see Cash and Bomber. I stare at Cash first. "Is everything sorted?"

Cash gives a clipped nod. "Sure is, Pres."

My heart races. I'm nervous about how Ava's going to react.

"Is Milly here yet?"

"I think she just pulled up."

"Get the word out to everyone. Do not let Ava go out the front."

He smirks. "I'll do it now."

When he leaves, my attention goes to Bomber. "What did you think about the meeting this morning with Graham?" Graham is the founder of Kings of Chaos.

"He had no issues with us shooting Jude. Did you know the prospect was Jude's nephew?"

"No, I didn't, but that Jude and him were stealing weed and dealing it on the side . . ." I shake my head and let out a low whistle. "I think he got let off too easy."

"I agree, but what are your thoughts about the future?" he asks, rubbing the side of his head with his hand. "Did you want to keep doing business with them?"

"We don't have a choice. We have to until we find another buyer."

Bomber takes a deep breath, a hint of a smile curving the edge of his lip. "Your woman can cook."

"Yes, she can," I reply with a smile. "You know . . . she thought you were celibate."

Bomber's mouth opens in disbelief.

"Don't worry, I set her straight," I taunt. "But she was worried that you would be lonely."

He stills. "Did you tell her about Zara?"

I playfully barge him with my shoulder, trying to lighten the mood. "Not my story to tell."

He subtly nods. His eyes peer off.

I wish I'd never brought it up. He really must have loved her to never want a relationship with a woman again. I never understood it, but now that I have Ava, I do because I could never see myself with anyone else. Even if something happens, I'd never be able to move on.

"Let's go get some breakfast."

As we walk through the house, it's quieter than usual, but then voices come from outside. I go to touch the back door handle, but I step back, letting Bomber go ahead while I go to the fridge and pull out the steak. I shake my head. I'm the alpha male here. I shouldn't have to give the dog a gourmet dinner for it to damn well like me.

I step toward the back door and open it. When I step outside, I see the men sitting at the tables and stuffing their mouths full of food. "Pancakes again?" I ask, then point to them. "My woman spoils all of you too much!"

Rage grins at me and Axle smiles with a mouthful of food, giving me the thumbs up.

I open the plastic covering the steak and reluctantly place it in Conan's bowl. He trots over and sits in front of it, drool oozing from his mouth. A part of me feels like making him wait for ages, but I don't.

"Eat," I tell him. When he does, I look at his leg in the plaster cast. "Well, at least you can't piss on me now."

As I walk over to Ava, I chuckle to myself. When I come up behind her, I bend down and kiss her cheek. "Hello, beautiful."

She blushes but flashes me one of her blinding smiles. "I'll get you a plate. How many pancakes do you want?"

"No, thanks. I'm saving myself for lunch," I reply. Really, my stomach is doing somersaults, worried about how she's going to respond. My hands rise to her shoulders and I massage them, enjoying the contented sigh that falls from her mouth.

Elena elbows Axle, who's beside her. "You don't rub my shoulders."

"Babe," he draws the word out while drilling displeased eyes into me. "Stop making me look bad," he says in a mocking tone.

I laugh as he turns back to his wife. "I'll rub your shoulders tonight. How about that?"

She smiles back. "You better!"

"A rub for a rub." He raises his eyebrow suggestively. Elena swats his chest as Ava's face screws up.

I lean down. "Don't listen to him," I whisper into her ear.

Her head falls back as she relaxes into the massage.

I love making Ava feel good. She's mine, and I will worship her every day for the rest of my life.

Ava

"Turn it up," I yell.

The volume of "Jump Around" by House of Pain gets so deafening I can feel the music. I sing, bopping to the lyrics, stirring the potato salad to go with the barbecue lunch. Viper slides into the kitchen like he's Tom Cruise in *Risky Business*, and he jumps around with me to the lyrics. Axle walks in, shaking his head at us but then breaks out dancing while raising his hands in the air. My heart is full as I laugh hysterically at them.

When the song finishes, Viper, Axle, and the sweet butts come in to help take the food outside onto the tables.

"Ava," Reaper calls, gesturing for me to go to him. I feel everyone's eyes on me as I make my way to him. Reaper searches the crowd but stops when he sees Rage. "You too. Come on, get up here."

The men cheer. Rage's eyes widen. He hesitates but then slowly makes his way over to us.

"Everyone, quiet," Reaper says to the men. "Today, we celebrate . . . our new patched-in member, Rage!" Cash passes Reaper Rage's new cut, and Reaper hands it to a frozen Rage, who looks shocked. But then the corner of his mouth curves into a smile showing all of his teeth.

I cheer and clap along with everyone. Rage puts his hands through the holes and pulls the vest up. It suits him.

Reaper shakes Rage's hand. "Welcome to the family." Reaper looks back at everyone. "But that's not it. We have two more things to celebrate."

I try to remember what else we're celebrating today. No one has mentioned anything. Cash passes another cut to Reaper, then Reaper turns to face me.

I look to the side of me, but no one is there. Reaper holds the vest out toward me. I stare at it until recognition flares in my eyes. It's mine.

"Now, don't get mad at me," he says in a charming voice.

There are no negative feelings toward the vest, not anymore. It means so much more than what I first thought the day I saw Elena's cut. It's the MC's tradition, and I want to be a part of that.

"I love you," he says with emotion in his voice. "And I want everyone to know that you're mine."

"I love you, too."

He holds the vest up to me as I slide my arms in both holes. Everyone cheers again, and I get a little teary but blink those pesky tears away. I examine the cut, my fingers traveling over the *Property of Reaper* patch.

I glance up at him. "Thank you." I rise on my toes to kiss him on the lips.

Elena rushes to me and hugs me, then leans back and points to both our vests. "Now we're matching," she says through a smile but then raises her hand. "I've got a surprise for you. I'll be back." She runs off.

Milly steps up next, puts her arms around me, and squeezes tight, then pulls back. "In biker terms, welcome to the White family."

"Thank you," I reply, my voice struggling to stay even.

Elena comes back with Conan, who is hobbling around with his plastered back leg. "Hey, Conan." His tail wags, and when he reaches me, I see a collar around his neck. It's leather, and on it is a patch that says *Property of Ava.* Next to it is the *War Brother's MC* logo. "This is amazing. Thank you!" I tell Elena.

Reaper steps to my side. "I've got a surprise for you too."

"Another one?" I ask in shock. Everyone laughs around us.

He puts his hand in mine, lacing our fingers together, pulling me along the side of the house, with everyone following us. When we get out the front of the clubhouse, there's a white SUV. "This is yours so you can drive to your course during the week."

I stand, speechless, my jaw on the ground. I glance up at him. "It's mine?"

He gives me a nod, then I abruptly leap into Reaper's arms. "It's beautiful. Oh my gosh."

"You got into your course?" Elena yells. "You never told me!"

I pull myself away from Reaper. "I opened the acceptance letter this morning."

Her hands fly to her mouth. Tears fall down her face, making my stomach drop. I step over to her. "Why are you crying?"

"Because you've come so far. I'm beyond proud of you, sis."

I blink furiously. "Stop crying! You'll make me cry. But know that I couldn't be where I am without you." My life isn't the same without her in it.

I peer back at Reaper. "If I only got accepted this morning, how did you organize the car so quickly?"

"I knew you would get in. We stored the car at Milly's house in the meantime."

I stare at the love of my life.

Being with him, I learned how to smile again. I no longer feel caged, because he's set me free.

The end.

Did you want to go into the draw to win a *free paperback*? Sign up for my mailing list. Simply opening my newsletter emails enters you to win any paperback.

If you love my books, please leave a *review* or *rating* on your purchased retailer or your favorite platform. It encourages other readers to take a chance on me. It truly makes a difference and provides crucial feedback.

SNEAK PEEK AT BOMBER

Bomber

"Is that a smile?"

I look up to see Viper walking toward me with a grin.

"You smiled!" he says, but my eyes narrow. He takes a seat beside me and playfully elbows me. "It's okay," he whispers. "It can be our little secret."

I push him. "Fuck off!"

He laughs. "Ohhh and defensive!" He blinks a few times, then his eyes widen. "It's that chick, isn't it?" He clicks his fingers. "What's her name . . ." He points at me. "Zara!"

I give him a clipped nod. "She's back in Crown Village."

He rubs his hands theatrically, true to form. "When can I meet her? I've been wanting to ever since you told me and Reaper about her."

I curse under my breath. "Look, I don't think you will." She probably won't even want to talk to me.

"You should have gone and seen her years ago when we got back from the military."

"I have seen her," I point out, though I know what he's talking about.

"No, like in person, instead of stalking her."

My lip twitches, though I try my best not to smile. "It's not stalking. I go a few times a year to check up on her. I like to know that she's doing okay."

I have resisted the urge to go to her and talk to her. But she's set up a new life, one without me in it. She doesn't come home because of her grief, and I could never ask her to stay in a place that strongly affects her. She seems a lot better than she was, and her well-being will always be more important than my own.

"Ah, yoo-hoo?"

I blink twice, Viper coming back into view. "Sorry, I was out of it."

"Women do that to ya."

I raise an eyebrow. "And how would you know? Have you even been in a relationship before?" I ask. Axle walks toward us.

Viper snorts. "I'm not stupid!"

Axle sits beside me with a wide smile, looking at Viper. "I strongly disagree."

Viper points to his patch. "I'm smart. See this patch? VP, motherfucker."

"That's because you love sucking Reaper's dick," Axle says, flicking his balled fist to his mouth in a jerking-off motion.

Viper's grin spreads. "You're a bastard!"

Axle laughs and slaps the table.

My lips mash together as I try not to laugh at these idiots.

Axle's jaw drops.

"What?" I ask.

He stands and leans over, touching my forehead with his

hand. "Are you feeling okay? Do you need to go to the hospital?"

I shove his hands off of me.

"He's smiling because he finally gets to see his girl," Viper says.

My eyes narrow at Viper's big mouth. Though I would give anything to call her mine.

"What girl?" Axle asks. He clears his throat, giving me a pointed look. "What girl?"

The only one.

All those years watching her from afar, now I can see her, touch her, and—if she can forgive me—be with her again.

After sparring with Viper, Axle, and Rage, I'm freshly showered and lying on my bed, thinking about Zara. I lived and breathed her. Who I was pales compared to what I have become. There's no going back because I can't erase the past, but every day away from her felt like I was dying a little each day.

I've missed the feel of Zara's silky hair cascading through my fingers, the scent of her perfume, and the taste of her lips. Everything about her. Each time I saw her, a pang of regret stung my chest, followed by self-loathing. I shouldn't regret putting her well-being above my own feelings, but every day without her has been a struggle.

After she left, my life revolved around the military, and now the MC. I have meaningless sex with escorts to fill the void.

Time may have moved on, but I haven't moved on from her. I can't, and I've never wanted to. Every time I left Zara to come back home to the MC, I consumed myself with work.

Being the sergeant at arms is easy because without Zara in my life, I have no heart or any real moral compass. I enjoy hurting others—it's a reprieve from my pain. That's what Demon and I have in common: fucked-up pasts. Demon is the enforcer, my right-hand man that protects patch members and the club.

The smell of cooked food wafts into my room. Reaper's ol' lady, Ava, can cook! I was unsure about her at the beginning, but despite how much pain she's been through with her ex-husband, she still is friendly to everyone. She reminds me of Zara.

I jump off the bed and grab my phone and wallet from the side table. I shove my wallet in my back pocket and swiftly head down the stairs to the kitchen. I inhale deeply, which makes my stomach growl.

I walk past the living room to see Elena, Axle, Viper, Candy, and Twitch watching TV. The echo of loud cracks gives me the impression the other men are outside practicing their shooting.

As I step into the kitchen, I lightly knock on the cupboard, aware of how jumpy Ava can get. But over time, she seems to have gotten more comfortable here. But I still don't want to trigger her.

She looks up at me and smiles.

"Do you know when dinner will be ready?"

"At least an hour. There's a big turkey in the oven."

I give her a chin lift, proceed through the house, and grab the keys to the van. I hope Zara likes the present I'm going to buy for her.

After dinner, there are conversations around the table. I lean in closer to Reaper. "I need to speak to you at some point."

He slowly nods. "I've been meaning to try these new cigars I got. How about we go out the back and talk?"

I rarely have a serious one-on-one conversation with Reaper because my life is the club, so I gather he knows what I've got to say is important to me.

"I'll meet you out there."

My chair squeaks against the wooden floor when I stand. I pick up my plate and go to the kitchen. Elena and the sweet butts are in there cleaning. I use my fork to scrape off a large portion of my food into the container for the dog.

Elena's eyes drop to my plate. "You didn't eat much."

I pause. Despite the awkward silence, I don't tell her why. She plasters on a smile, reaches for my plate, and takes it from me.

I move to the back door and open it, but I'm met with resistance. I shove it harder. The door opens wide. Conan, Ava's dog, stands there. Judging by the drool hanging from his mouth, he must be able to smell the food. The door shuts behind me, and as I'm walking to the table outside, I look over my shoulder. Conan is sitting outside the door, patiently waiting for Ava to feed him.

Shortly after, the back door opens and Reaper walks through, stops at Conan, and shakes his head. "Rottweilers shouldn't be that fat. Is he getting bigger or what?" Reaper asks as he strolls toward me with a box in his hand.

My eyes skim over Conan's gut. "He has put on more weight."

"I keep telling Ava to stop feeding him so much."

I wait until he sits beside me. "I don't think it's just Ava."

His brows furrow. "What do you mean?"

"Everyone feeds the dog, and most people also give him

snacks throughout the day. I know because I've sat here and watched."

I like this spot outside. Trees surround us, the air is fresh, and it's quiet. It's relaxing. I hate being confined indoors.

"Are Viper and Rage still taking the dog for runs?"

"Yes, but the dog gets fed all day and at night."

The back door opens again. Ava comes out with a massive container of scraps and places them in Conan's bowl.

"Sit," she says in what is supposed to be a commanding voice, but she's too softly spoken for it to sound like that. "Eat."

"Beautiful, your dog's getting too fat. I think you need to stop feeding him so much."

Ava lifts her gaze to us. She smiles. "No, I think we need to get another dog."

"Another one?" Reaper pipes up. "One is more than enough."

She quirks a brow, then walks back inside.

"She's getting another dog, isn't she?" I ask, my voice tinged with amusement.

"I fucking hope not." He pulls out a cigar and uses a cutter to slice the cap off. After lighting it, he hands it to me.

I bring it to my mouth and draw in, savoring the taste, before blowing out the smoke.

"Zara's back in Crown Village."

"Has it really been ten years?" he asks, surprised. "I remember you telling us about her."

I sigh. "So much has happened in that time. I just wanted to let you know if I'm out of it or not myself. It's because she's back in town."

The next day, I lie in bed. I didn't sleep well last night. I've been in a daze, going through the motions. I can't get Zara out of my head. All I can think about is she probably hates me, but I hate myself more for lying to her about the real reason I broke up with her. I've lived with regret ever since.

I didn't want to break up with her, but I had pressure from her family to do the right thing by her. I was the only one keeping her here. It came down to her safety and well-being. Even though I was selfish and wanted to keep her, I knew if something ever happened to her, I'd never forgive myself.

Grab your copy of <u>Bomber</u> now.

If you prefer a romantic comedy, Viper's story follows on from Bomber.

RESOURCES

One Australian dollar of every paperback book purchase from Bianca's website will go to the LifeLine charity.

If you are struggling with your mental health, contact Life-Line. LifeLine is available in many countries and offers help for people experiencing emotional distress. They provide confidential crisis support, and in most instances, you can call, chat online, or text.

Please visit https://lifeline-intl.com/our-network/ for more information.

If you are seeking help with a drinking problem, contact Alcoholics Anonymous. AA is an informal society that operates in many countries and offers peer support for recovery from alcoholism.

Please visit https://www.aa.org/find-aa/world for more information.

ACKNOWLEDGMENTS

To Heavenly Dad,
I miss you every day, but I'm thankful for having you in my life.

There are plenty of people who helped me make this book what it is. A big thank you to my Mumma, who is my biggest supporter, for always being there and taking time out to listen on the phone, to the chaos that is my life. If anyone wants to know who I learnt my potty mouth from, that would be my mum, Carol. I will no doubt get a playful smack from telling all my readers. 😊

Since I was born, we owned show championship rottweilers. They meant the world to my dad, so I wanted to show a different side of the breed that not everyone gets to see. The protective, loyal, sweet, and cheeky side.

To Merredy, my partner in crime, Brydie, my meme bestie, and Emma, the sweetheart. I love that, no matter how much time passes, our friendships always pick up where they left off. Thank you for always being there!

To Nicole and the beta readers, thank you for helping me make the story what it is today. Nicole, I'm forever grateful for your opinions. I value your input, and I get a kick out of your genuine excitement every time you get to read the first draft—even though it's rough.

Thank you to Emily from Quirky Circe for your vision and stunning design work for both book covers and to the editors for their feedback, direction, and insight. I appreciate your patience with my terrible ability at meeting deadlines. And let's be honest: you have your work cut out for you with grammar on my manuscript.

And to the readers and bloggers, from the bottom of my heart, thank you for taking the time to read, share, and review my book.

Until next time,

Bianca Lee Ward

ABOUT THE AUTHOR

Bianca Lee Ward is an Australian romance author with a love of culinary adventures and a playlist for every mood. She enjoys exploring themes of identity, personal growth, and resilience in her work—with a little spice on the side. When she isn't lost in storytelling or absorbed in her latest read, Bianca can be found watching true crime stories and documentaries.

You can connect with Bianca online at:
Website: www.biancaleeward.com
Email: info@biancaleeward.com
Instagram: https://www.instagram.com/biancaleeward
Facebook: https://www.facebook.com/biancaleeward
Spotify: Bianca Lee Ward
Pinterest: https://www.pinterest.com.au/biancaleeward
Goodreads: https://www.goodreads.com/author/show/
30477361.Bianca_Lee_Ward
Bookbub: https://www.bookbub.com/authors/bianca-lee-ward

Don't forget to sign up to Bianca's mailing list, where you'll get *huge* discounts, *exclusive* giveaways, and new release alerts!

www.ingramcontent.com/pod-product-compliance
Lightning Source LLC
Chambersburg PA
CBHW061121100726
47911CB00013B/626